## PRAISE FOR WILLIAM WENTON AND THE IMPOSSIBLE PUZZLE (BOOK 1):

2017 PARENTS' CHOICE AWARD WINNER

"Part Alex Rider, part Artemis Fowl, part *Da Vinci Code* for kids, this title will captivate action and mystery enthusiasts."
**—SLJ**

"This series opener is a gripping story from early on, and the wonky twists and turns ramp up the excitement as readers learn more about William's family and this crazy metal at the core of the drama."
**—BCCB**

"Peers' first novel follows the pattern of many such school and adventure stories—think Hogwarts with robots and carnivorous robotic plants—but there are plenty of twists to keep readers guessing."
**—BOOKLIST**

## PRAISE FOR WILLIAM WENTON AND THE SECRET PORTAL (BOOK 2):

"William Wenton is back in a new adventure packed with peril. The adventure leads to the Himalayas, a portal between worlds, a hint of unknown history, and tragedy. Not all is lost, however, and the stage is set for another adventure. Peers maintains a brisk pace throughout, and William and his friends are just as appealing as before."
**—BOOKLIST**

# SOLVE THE PUZZLE!

# WILLIAM WENTON AND THE SECRET PORTAL

Translated from the Norwegian by Tara Chace

## BOBBIE PEERS

**Aladdin**

New York  London  Toronto  Sydney  New Delhi

**ALADDIN**

An imprint of Simon & Schuster Children's Publishing Division
1230 Avenue of the Americas, New York, New York 10020
First Aladdin paperback edition July 2019
Text copyright © 2016 by by H. Aschehoug & Co. (W. Nygaard), Oslo
English language translation copyright © 2018 by Tara Chace
Originally published in Norway by H. Aschehoug & Co. as *Kryptalportalen*
Jacket illustration of type, gears, and mountain copyright © 2018 by Luke Lucas
Jacket illustration of boy and girl copyright © 2018 by Eric Deschamps
Also available in an Aladdin hardcover edition.
All rights reserved, including the right of reproduction in whole or in part in any form.
ALADDIN and related logo are registered trademarks of Simon & Schuster, Inc.
For information about special discounts for bulk purchases, please contact Simon & Schuster
Special Sales at 1-866-506-1949 or business@simonandschuster.com.
The Simon & Schuster Speakers Bureau can bring authors to your live event.
For more information or to book an event, contact the Simon & Schuster Speakers Bureau
at 1-866-248-3049 or visit our website at www.simonspeakers.com.
Book designed by Jessica Handelman
The text of this book was set in Bembo.
Manufactured in the United States of America 0619 OFF
2 4 6 8 10 9 7 5 3 1
The Library of Congress has cataloged the hardcover edition as follows:
Names: Peers, Bobbie, author. | Chace, Tara, translator.
Title: William Wenton and the secret portal / by Bobbie Peers ;
translated from the Norwegian by Tara Chace. Other titles: Kryptalportalen. English
Description: First Aladdin hardcover edition. | New York : Aladdin, 2018. |
Series: William Wenton ; 2 | Originally published in Norwegian in 2017 under title: Kryptalportalen. |
Summary: Code-breaking genius William Wenton returns to the Institute for Post-Human
Research in hopes of discovering why the intelligent metal luridium in his body seems
to be causing seizures, but while there he encounters secrets, increased security, and
threats from an enemy he thought was frozen in the basement.
Identifiers: LCCN 2017053743 | ISBN 9781481478281 (hc) | ISBN 9781481478304 (eBook)
Subjects: | CYAC: Ciphers—Fiction. | Puzzles—Fiction. | Mystery and detective stories. |
Science fiction. | BISAC: JUVENILE FICTION / Mysteries & Detective Stories. |
JUVENILE FICTION / Humorous Stories. | JUVENILE FICTION / Fantasy & Magic.
Classification: LCC PZ7.1.P4397 Wil 2018 |
DDC [Fic]—dc23
LC record available at https://lccn.loc.gov/2017053743
ISBN 9781481478298 (pbk)

*To Daniel. You inspire me.*

## DEPOSITORY FOR
## IMPOSSIBLE ARCHAEOLOGY

**Pontus Dippel positioned his forehead against the scanner** next to the elevator.

He wanted to do one last pass before he left for the night. The items downstairs, collected from all corners of the globe, were some of the rarest and most valuable artifacts in the world. Now they were safely stored in the Depository for Impossible Archaeology beneath the Institute for Post-Human Research.

A green beam flashed across his forehead, and the elevator doors slid open with a ding. Pontus entered, and two guard-bots wheeled in behind him as the doors closed.

When the elevator doors opened again, he was deep underground. He proceeded down a long hallway, stopping in front of a steel-clad security door. Neither Pontus nor the guard-bots noticed a dark figure materializing behind them.

Pontus placed his forehead on another scanner.

"Welcome," a computerized voice said.

The door slid open with a quiet swish.

Suddenly one of the guard-bots said: "HALT!"

Pontus whipped around and spotted a figure coming toward them.

The dark hallway made it hard to see. But it was a woman. Her black, uncombed hair was draped like tentacles over part of her face, and yellow teeth snarled inside a grinning mouth. Something on her left hand glinted in the dim light.

"HALT!" the guard-bot said again.

But the woman continued onward. Then, with one swift movement, she raised her arm, and a beam shot out, vaporizing the two robots.

"No, it can't be . . . ," Pontus said, raising his hands in front of himself. "It's not possible. You're supposed to be . . . dead!"

Pontus shook his head as he backed away into the dark room.

The woman followed, closing the door behind them.

# 1

William looked up at a red lamp in the ceiling. Bold letters on the lamp read LIVE. He could feel the heat radiating from the powerful stage lights nearby.

He glanced over at a stressed-out woman wearing a headset. She stood not far from him while busy workers passed behind her, carrying large cables and more stage lights. William kept his gaze on her. When she gave him the thumbs-up, it would be his turn.

His first appearance on TV.

Never in his wildest dreams had he imagined that he would find himself in a situation like this. It was as if everything had turned upside down now. After living under a secret name at an undisclosed address for most of his life, it now felt as though everyone knew who he was, or at least that they'd heard his name.

And tonight, because he had solved the world's most difficult code, he was going to be on national TV. Slowly he was being turned into a celebrity. And he wasn't sure he liked it.

The woman with the headset gave him the thumbs-up.

He heard applause from behind the stage wall and people calling his name. There was something menacing about hundreds of people he didn't know shouting his name. William froze.

"William Wenton . . . where are you?" he heard the host's voice calling from the stage. "Maybe he found some code back there that he had to crack first."

The audience laughed.

Someone started chanting his name: "Will-yum . . . Will-yum . . ."

Soon, hundreds of voices were chanting in unison: "WILL-YUM . . . WILL-YUM . . . WILL-YUM . . ."

People clapped and stomped their feet.

The headset woman rushed toward him, motioning for him to get moving. She didn't look pleased. William took a deep breath and slipped through an opening between two of the stage walls. He stopped as the bright lights hit his face. The audience burst into enthusiastic cheers. He tried to look around, but he was completely blinded by the spotlights.

"This way!" the host's voice said from somewhere in the light.

As William began to walk, he caught his foot on a cable and fell flat on his face.

A few people gasped.

But there was one person who laughed.

William recognized the laugh right away. It belonged to Vektor Hansen, a self-professed genius and master code breaker. The same self-professed genius whom William had beaten by solving the Impossible Puzzle, the world's most difficult code. And now Vektor Hansen was laughing so hard he could barely catch his breath.

William maneuvered his foot free and stood up.

"I hope you're insured," the chubby host said, waddling over to help him.

William looked in confusion at Ludo Kläbbert, whose whitened teeth beamed in a broad grin. William hadn't seen Ludo since the man had served as the emcee at the Impossible Exhibit, where William had cracked the code that turned his life upside down.

Ludo led William over to a sofa and gestured for the boy to sit. Vektor Hansen stopped laughing the instant their eyes met. He became serious and stared at William through narrowed eyes, then scooted over to put as much room between himself and William as possible.

Ludo slipped around behind a desk and plunked himself

back into his seat. He sat there and smiled at them for a while.

William glanced over at the two TV cameras rolling across the floor in front of them. One of them was pointed right at him, and he could see himself on a screen at the side of the stage. He'd always had pale skin, but he looked extra washed out now in the bright lights.

"So how does it feel, William . . . sitting here with the man you so epically humiliated a few months ago?" Ludo asked.

William glanced over at Vektor, who had his arms and legs crossed. His body language made his loathing of William very clear.

William knew that he had never tried to humiliate anyone.

"How does it feel?" Ludo repeated impatiently.

"I don't know," William said. "I mean, I didn't mean to break the code."

"'Didn't mean to break the code,'" Vektor said. "How can someone solve a code that difficult without even wanting to?"

"Vektor has a point," Ludo said, looking at William. "How could you possibly have solved the Impossible Puzzle . . . by accident?"

William couldn't think of anything to say, so he stayed silent.

In his own defense, he could have told them about the luridium. That 49 percent of his body consisted of this high-tech supermetal. A metal that allowed him to solve difficult codes in a trancelike state.

"He probably knew the solution beforehand," Vektor said, squinting at William.

"Is that true, William?" Ludo followed up. "Did you already know the answer?"

"No . . . I didn't know the answer," William said. He glanced out at the audience, who were sitting on the edge of their seats in rapt attention. "That's the truth. I didn't know anything. It just . . . happened."

They sat in icy silence for what seemed like forever. Then Ludo clapped his hands and grinned.

"We can't get so carried away that we forget why we're really here." Ludo laughed, leaping out of his chair and pointing at the studio audience. "Are you ready to get started?"

The audience broke into boisterous applause.

"Are you ready for a challenge?" Ludo asked, now pointing at William.

"Um . . ." William hesitated. No one had told him about a challenge.

"Great," Ludo cheered, snapping his chubby fingers in the air.

A woman with a stiff smile and wearing a long silver dress appeared from behind the stage wall. She was pushing a serving cart, and on it was a big silver platter with a shiny lid covering it.

William wondered what the lid could be hiding. It could be anything, but he knew it would be related to codes somehow.

Ludo turned to the audience. "Are you ready?" he cried, and pointed to the percussionist in the house orchestra beside the stage. An enthusiastic drumroll made the air in the hot studio vibrate. The audience started cheering again.

"What do you say?" Ludo shouted to the audience. "Should we give Vektor Hansen another shot?"

The audience responded with a YESSS! so loud the floor trembled.

"Do you want to see what's underneath the lid?" Ludo pointed at the lid on the cart.

"YEEEEEEAH!!" the audience yelled, even louder.

And with a dramatic gesture, Ludo grabbed the handle on the lid and whipped it off.

A gasp ran through the studio audience.

William couldn't believe his eyes. There were two colorful cardboard boxes about the size of shoe boxes on the platter. THE DIFFICULTY glimmered at him in large gold letters on the front. Under the letters was a plastic window revealing the contents: an oblong, metallic cylinder that looked like the Impossible Puzzle—the puzzle William had beaten Vektor Hansen in solving.

"Do you see what that looks like?" Ludo said, smiling at William.

Ludo picked up one box so the audience could see it too.

"These will be for sale in every toy store in the country tomorrow," he said. An excited gasp ran through the crowd.

William was dumbstruck. He looked at the remaining box on the platter. He couldn't believe it. A toy version of the Impossible Puzzle.

"Who wants to see two of the world's best code breakers compete to see who can solve the Difficulty the fastest?"

The audience burst into raucous applause.

William glanced over at Vektor, who was sitting at his end of the sofa, smirking. Did people really want the two of them to compete at solving something that was going to be sold in *toy stores*?

Ludo Kläbbert raised his hands to signal the audience to be quiet. Then he turned to William. "Well, what do you say, William? Are you ready for a challenge?"

William looked over at the audience. Then at Hansen. He felt trapped. No one had told him there would be a competition. Vektor grinned at him, and William got the feeling that the man had known all about this. William had been tricked into this, and now there was no way out.

"But they're not . . . real—" William said.

"Wonderful," Ludo cut him off. "And what do you say, Vektor?"

Vektor removed his leather vest and gave his ponytail a toss. "I'm always ready for a good puzzle." He cracked his fingers.

"The rules are simple," Ludo said. "The first one to solve the Difficulty is the winner."

Ludo nodded to the woman in the silver dress. She opened the boxes and set both cylinders on the table in front of the two contestants. Ludo raised his arms as if he were about to start a drag race and then glanced at the audience. Then he turned to William and Vektor.

"Are you ready?"

Vektor nodded.

Once again, William was about to protest, but he stopped himself. Yes, he had been tricked into something he didn't want to do, but this was the situation he was in now. . . . In a split second, he adjusted his mind, looked at the puzzle in front of him, and nodded. "I'm ready!"

"GREAT," Ludo shouted, then started counting. "THREE . . . TWO . . . ONE!" His chubby arms lingered for a couple of seconds, then dropped as he cried, "GO!"

In a flash Vektor snatched the cylinder in front of him.

William did the same. He could tell right away that the toy wasn't the same high quality as the Impossible Puzzle. Most of the pieces were plastic, and the device was a lot lighter. Small squares that could be moved up and down divided the cylinder. Inside each square was a small symbol. William would have to move the squares around in a specific order until he had solved the code.

William glanced over at Hansen, who was already well

under way. His long fingers flew over the device, twisting and turning the cylinder. Vektor was so engrossed in what he was doing that a drop of drool had started to develop on his lower lip.

William closed his eyes and concentrated, the way he always did when he was code breaking. He sat for a bit and waited for the luridium in his body to take over.

Then he felt it.

That unique sensation he always got. It started with a tingling in his stomach and then moved up his spine and out into his hands.

It was like everything around him disappeared. William saw only the cylinder he held in his hands. It was as if it began to glow before it seemed to come apart, the various sections floating up into the air in front of him. William knew this wasn't really happening. Only he could see it. This was how the luridium in his body helped him organize the codes he solved. It was like some other force gave him the answers to the codes he wanted to solve, but then he had to do all the work. William looked at the floating symbols as they twirled and looped in front of him. Like they were trying to rearrange themselves. And in a way, they were. Then a pattern started to form in their movements. Some of the symbols moved upward, others sideways. William looked down at the cylinder and started moving the little squares around, mimicking the movements of the floating symbols.

Faster and faster his hands moved.

They twisted and turned the various sections of the cylinder at breakneck pace. And he knew that he was going to win. Nothing could stop him now.

A bright flash of light shot in front of his eyes. At first he thought someone had pointed one of the monstrous stage lights directly on his face, but then the light split up and formed little lightning bolts. It felt like they were inside his head. They darted around like a swarm of confused stars. And before he knew it . . . they were gone. Leaving only darkness behind.

Pain exploded in his head like a bomb, and he felt his body go limp.

Something was wrong.

His fingers were shaking uncontrollably. He could hardly hold on to the Difficulty, and the glow that had surrounded it an instant before was gone.

Something was *very* wrong.

His whole body started shaking, and he couldn't control it anymore. His hands were so cold he could hardly feel them.

Then an image flashed in front of his eyes. It was like he was standing in a large cave where a huge glowing golden ring levitated in front of him.

And then William was back in the TV studio.

He looked down at the cylinder. He tried to hold on, but the cylinder slipped out of his numb fingers and dropped to the floor as if in slow motion. William watched in shock as the device hit the floor and shattered.

He stared in confusion at all the pieces lying on the floor in front of him.

The Difficulty was broken.

William looked up and then out at the audience. He could see people leaning over and whispering to each other. He reached for his head and looked up at Hansen, who was holding the two pieces of his toy up in triumph.

It had split in two. He'd solved it.

Hansen started hopping around like a deranged kangaroo, gloating: "I WON! I WON! I BEAT WILLIAM WENTON!"

# 2

**William sat at his desk.**

He looked down at the metal cube he was holding in his hands. Strange symbols covered the entire surface. William pushed one of the symbols, it made a loud click, and the cube started vibrating. That meant that William had managed to solve it. He placed the cube on the desk in front of him. It was the last in a bunch of mechanical puzzles William had solved that night.

After his devastating defeat at the TV studio, he had gone straight home and up to his room. He had spent the rest of the night solving one code after another without any problems. Most of the codes that sat on the desk in front of him now were many times more difficult than that stupid toy.

What had happened at the studio? What had made his body shake that way? And what was that glowing ring that he had seen? The questions were piling up quickly.

William leaned back in his chair and looked out the window. Outside, there was only darkness. He felt tired but knew that he wouldn't be able to sleep. He wondered what his grandfather was doing right now and where he was. William hadn't heard a peep from him since he had left on a secret trip. And that was almost three months ago.

He leaned over and opened one of the drawers in the large wooden desk his grandfather had given him. He reached inside and lifted out something that looked like a metal crab. It was about the size of a dinner plate. William put it in front of him on the desk. The robot crab was part of a school assignment his teacher Mr. Humburger had given him. William had been working on the crab for weeks now, and it was almost done, but it still needed a few minor adjustments. William leaned over and grabbed a screwdriver from the desk and got to work.

A few hours later William was sitting at the kitchen table.

He hadn't slept a wink all night, and his head felt like it was stuffed with cotton.

His mom stood with her back to him. She was making pancakes. She always made pancakes when William was feeling down. He looked over at a folded newspaper that was sitting on the table. The headline, in all caps, read WILLIAM WENTON: NOT SO BRILLIANT AFTER ALL. Underneath, there was a picture of the euphoric Vektor Hansen holding up his solved Difficulty, while William sat on the TV-studio sofa in a daze.

"Look . . . you can eat as many as you want," his mother said, setting a plate with a mountain of pancakes in front of him.

William shrugged. He didn't know which was worse: his defeat in a competition everyone had expected him to win, or the sensation he'd had of losing control of his body.

What was it that had come over him? Could it be some kind of medical condition? Epilepsy? Migraine? Brain seizure? He considered telling his mother. But she had been through enough these last years, and he didn't want to worry her. He hoped that the seizure would be a onetime thing, and that it wouldn't come back.

His mother noticed the newspaper on the table. She snatched it up and stuffed it under a pile of old papers on the kitchen counter. Then she turned to William and stood there watching him as he ate.

"Are you okay?" she said.

"Yeah," William lied. "Why?"

"It's just . . ." She paused, as if she wanted to plan her words carefully. "On TV . . . you seemed a little strange. Like something was wrong . . ."

"I'm okay, Mom," William said, and forced a smile.

His mother jumped when something crashed out in the hallway. It sounded as if someone had dropped a piano down the stairs.

"He's starting to get the hang of it," she said, smiling. She seemed relieved to finally have something else to talk about.

"Mm-hmm . . ." William looked toward the door.

Then they heard another bang followed by a loud crash. His mother hurried out into the hallway.

"Is everything okay?" he heard her ask.

"Yeah. . . . It's a minor calibration issue," his dad said.

"Do you need any help?"

"Everything's fine!" his father said, followed by a couple of thumps and the sound of breaking glass.

"I never liked that vase anyway," his mother said as she backed into the kitchen again.

William straightened up. Heavy footsteps approached out in the hallway.

His father appeared in the doorway and continued at high speed into the kitchen.

"Hi, William," was all he managed as he fixed his eyes on the empty chair next to William. "I can do this," he said, gritting his teeth as he staggered toward the chair like a toddler.

He had metallic braces attached to the outsides of his

legs. The braces ran all the way from his hips down to his feet and were secured with Velcro straps at the ankles.

William's father was wearing a partial exoskeleton. William knew the prefix "exo" came from Greek and meant "outside." He'd watched a lot of nature shows about animals with exoskeletons. Beetles, for example.

The contraption had been delivered to their door a few weeks before from the Institute for Post-Human Research and addressed to his father. An accompanying letter said that the exoskeleton was a new prototype they wanted him to test. It made it possible for people like William's father to get around without a wheelchair. William knew that the Institute was trying to make a supersuit that would give the wearer superhuman strength and endurance. A great thing to wear when one was out in the field, searching through dangerous caves and jungles for hidden archeological arti-facts and ancient codes.

In the beginning his father had flat out refused. He didn't want anything to do with the exoskeleton or the Institute, and he'd wanted to send it back right away. But in the end William's mother had managed to convince him to give it a try first. She might have been regretting that now. Their house looked like a herd of stampeding buffalo had stormed through it.

William's dad stomped across the kitchen floor and crashed into the refrigerator. He tipped backward, hitting the kitchen counter and causing the fridge to wobble.

"It's fine . . . it's fine," William's dad said, grabbing the kitchen curtains.

The refrigerator door swung open, and a carton of milk toppled out. The milk glugged out across the floor, making it even harder for his father to remain standing.

"I'll wipe that up," William's mother said.

His father let go of the curtains and glanced over at William. His face looked tense, but there was a hint of a smile.

"How are you doing today?" his dad asked in a strained voice as he staggered toward the table.

"Okay," William lied again, setting a pancake on his plate.

His dad flopped onto the chair next to him. "Mmm, pancakes," he said, helping himself to three of them from the stack. Then he looked at William.

"Don't worry about what happened yesterday. We know you're the best code breaker in the world," he said with a forced smile.

Hearing his father say those words helped. A year earlier his dad had been so opposed to codes that he'd forbidden William from studying cryptology. But after the Institute had saved William from Abraham Talley, his father had slowly warmed up to the fact that William had code breaking in his blood. Just like his grandfather. And right now William felt good having a father who believed in him and backed him up. Even if he was wrong. William had tried to solve a toy puzzle, and he'd lost fair and square. There was no escaping that, and his self-esteem had suffered a major blow.

Now he feared that the luridium that kept him alive, and made him a code genius, was malfunctioning. He had to get in touch with his grandfather. He would know what to do. And he had to get back to the Institute for Post-Human Research. They could find out what was wrong with him.

# 3

**Mr. Humburger stood in front of the class, his arms folded,** staring at them with his catlike eyes.

William glanced at his teacher's sizeable belly. He could almost hear it counting down before it exploded and annihilated them all.

"Did everyone complete their assignment?"

Twenty heads nodded in unison.

"William? Do you have anything to show us?" Mr. Humburger asked, giving him a cold stare. "Or have you been too busy making a fool of yourself on live TV?" He chuckled, a laugh that ended as abruptly as it had begun.

Mr. Humburger had never thought much of William. He didn't seem to like students who were smarter than him. And he didn't like the fact that William was now called one of the world's best code breakers.

"Did everyone get to see William's somewhat clumsy TV appearance yesterday?" Mr. Humburger asked the whole class.

Everyone nodded.

"Great." Mr. Humburger chuckled before turning his eyes back to William. "I hope what happened has made you a little less interested in codes, and more set on making an effort at school?"

William didn't answer. After yesterday's events he already felt quite beaten, so he couldn't show any signs of weakness. If he did, Mr. Humburger would use every opportunity to break him down even further.

"Did you finish your assignment, William? Did you bring a project to present in front of the class?"

William glanced down at his backpack on the floor next to his desk. Of course he'd done his homework. He'd finished the mechanical crab. It was one of the coolest things he'd made in a long time.

"Well?" Mr. Humburger approached William with cat-like footsteps and stopped in front of his desk.

William glanced at Mr. Humburger's big belly, which was wobbling right in front of his face like a blob of jelly.

"He brought something! It's in his backpack," said a freckled girl who sat right behind him. She pointed to a thin metal leg that protruded up from William's backpack. The leg jerked and wiggled. William regretted even bringing the crab to school. Right now, he just needed people to leave him alone.

"Well, let's see it, then!"

William looked down at his backpack again. Now a second leg had appeared. It looked like the crab was on its way up anyway, so he reached down and carefully pulled it out and placed it on his desk.

"It's a prototype, and fragile . . ." William didn't have a chance to say any more before Mr. Humburger grabbed the crab.

"Well, what have we here?" Mr. Humburger mumbled, holding the metallic crab up in front of his face for a closer look.

"It looks like a crab," Mr. Humburger said after examining it. He looked at William. "What does it do? Besides being some kind of mechanical . . . thing."

Mr. Humburger knocked on the shell with his knuckles. The crab twitched and tried to wiggle free from his grip.

"It's a feisty one," Mr. Humburger said, and looked at William again. "Are you going to show us what it can do, or not?"

"Can I have it back now?" William said. He didn't like the way Mr. Humburger was handling the crab.

"Of course you can have it back," Mr. Humburger said.

"After you've shown us what it does." Mr. Humburger turned on his heel and returned to his desk.

William stood up and walked to the teacher's desk.

"Think fast," Mr. Humburger yelled, tossing the crab to him.

William caught the robot in midair and held it in both hands. He didn't want to risk Mr. Humburger grabbing it from him again.

"Please explain what you've made," Mr. Humburger said. His desk creaked as he sat on the edge.

William turned around to face the class. "Sandy is a mechanical crab . . . ," he began, holding the crab up. "It can do several things. It can walk, it can climb, and it can fetch things."

"Can it, now?" Mr. Humburger's chubby face contorted into a malicious grin. "Show us, then. . . ." It was clear that Mr. Humburger didn't have any faith in William's invention.

William set the crab on the desk.

The little crab stood there without moving. William gave it a gentle nudge with his index finger, but nothing happened.

"Great work, William." Mr. Humburger smiled.

A few of the students laughed. A tall, thin boy, who happened to be Mr. Humburger's favorite, snickered loudly.

William glanced at the crab again. He wanted to grab it and run out of the room. But he didn't.

The crab's legs started scuttling, and the crab raced toward the edge of the desk. A gasp ran through the class.

"Catch it! It's going to fall," one of the girls yelped, pointing at the crab, which was moving at full speed. As the crab got to the edge, it stopped and changed directions.

"It knows when to turn around," William said, looking up at the class.

Most the students looked impressed now, and William felt a little better.

"What else can it do?" Mr. Humburger said, glancing at his watch. "Besides move its feet. Each presentation lasts three minutes. You have thirty-eight seconds left to show us something other than a windup toy."

"Sometimes it can climb up walls." William swallowed dryly. Why was Mr. Humburger always picking on him like this?

"Sounds too good to be true," his teacher said.

"It is true!" said William. Now he wanted to show the class everything his crab could do.

He set it on the floor, and the crab shuffled sideways until it hit the wall at the other end of the room.

"Time's up," Mr. Humburger said. "Collect the crab and return to your seat."

William started toward the crab but stopped as a gasp ran through the class.

"Look!" a girl shouted, pointing at the crab, which was

already halfway up the wall. Tiny sparks flew off its metal legs as it moved upward.

William seized the moment.

"It has a static-electricity generator in its belly," he explained. "That's the same as when you rub a balloon against your hair and then it sticks to the wall."

The whole class stared at the crab, which scrabbled sideways up the wall until it reached the corner. It sat there for a little while before proceeding upside down across the ceiling.

"It hasn't done that before," William mumbled.

"What?" Mr. Humburger said.

"That!" William pointed at the crab. "Walked upside down."

Everyone's eyes followed the mechanical crab as it darted back and forth on the ceiling. Then finally it crashed into a lamp and came to a halt . . . directly over Mr. Humburger. The lamp cracked, and one of the crab's legs disappeared into the glass.

William's heart almost stopped as sparks appeared from inside the lamp and the lights in the classroom blinked menacingly.

"Do something!" Mr. Humburger shouted, and pointed a chubby finger at William. "It's short-circuiting the whole school."

William looked around. He had to get the crab away

from the lamp. His eyes landed on a long-handled broom in one of the corners. He ran over, grabbed it, and stood under the crab.

As William raised the broom, Mr. Humburger yanked it from him and started poking at the crab.

"It's stuck," Mr. Humburger said, poking the crab even harder.

The crab fell off the ceiling and dropped down onto Mr. Humburger's head. The class gasped in surprise as the lights in the room blinked and died out.

"It attacked me!" Mr. Humburger shouted. He looked around in fear, grabbing his head and tottering around in the semidarkness.

"There it is!" one of the boys said, pointing at the crab, which lay on the floor behind Mr. Humburger. Smoke bellowed out from a crack in the metal shell.

"It's on fire," Mr. Humburger shouted, and started whacking the crab with the business end of the broom.

"Stop," William shouted.

But Mr. Humburger didn't stop. He continued whacking the crab harder and harder.

William felt a stabbing pain in his head and a paralyzing cold spreading through his body and arms. Little dots of light appeared in front of him, and a high-pitched sound, so loud it felt like his head was about to explode, rang in his ears.

He glanced down at his hands, which felt as cold as ice. They were trembling. This attack was like the one he'd had in the TV studio the day before, but it was much stronger.

William looked over at Mr. Humburger, who was still whacking the defenseless crab. And he knew one thing: He had to get out of there.

It was like a bad dream. The kind where you try to run but can't move. A bright light flashed across his vision. And for a brief moment he was in the cave again, standing under the floating ring.

Then he was back in the classroom.

William battled his way over to Mr. Humburger, grabbed the crab, and continued toward the door.

He could hear Mr. Humburger shouting something behind him. But most of his hearing was gone, and the shouts sounded like they were underwater, distant and scrambled.

The only thing that mattered now was getting out of there.

# 4

**William stopped on the sidewalk outside the school yard to** catch his breath.

His heart was chugging like a steam locomotive. He looked down at the crab in his hand. The smoke had ceased, and the little metal body was completely still. His hands had stopped shaking, and the seizure had subsided. He was in control of his body again, but he was still shaken. What on earth was happening to him?

He had to get away from the school, find some place where he could think.

He placed the crab inside his jacket and started walking.

"William . . . ," a hoarse voice said. It was almost as if the voice had come from inside his head.

William stopped and looked around.

He noticed a dark figure standing in the shadow of a bus stop a little distance away. The figure stood so still that it almost merged into the background. It was a woman with black shoulder-length hair covering part of her face.

She was wearing a black velvet jacket with metal buttons, a hood, and long sleeves. She had on purple pants and boots that stopped right under her knees. She wore a black leather glove on her left hand. William caught a faint whiff of something that smelled like burned rubber.

"You're trembling. Is everything okay?" the figure asked in perfect English. Again, it felt like the voice came from inside William's head. Alarmed, he brought his hand to his ear.

"William," the woman continued. "Are you okay?" This time her voice came from her and no longer inside his head.

"How do you know my name?" William asked, dropping his hand.

A stupid question, since he'd just appeared on national TV, but it felt like a natural thing to ask.

The figure took a couple of steps closer to William, who instinctively pulled back a little.

"Gotta go," he said. He turned around and started walking away.

"Wait," the figure said.

William didn't wait. He sped up. Something told him

that it was a good idea to get away from this woman as soon as possible. After he'd walked for a while, he cast a quick glance behind him.

The figure was gone, but he kept moving.

Then he spotted her again. She was standing on the sidewalk about ten yards in front of him.

William stopped.

He stood there bewildered. No one could run that fast. It was impossible.

"I need you to come with me, William," the woman said.

"Who are you?" William asked. His eyes scanned the surroundings for an escape route.

"You'll find out soon enough," she said, and removed the leather glove. Her hand was mechanical. Like a robot hand, but a very old one. It seemed to be made out of copper or brass. William could see little gears and wheels and blinking buttons on the wrist as well as something that looked like a round pressure gauge. The mechanical fingers clicked as they moved.

The woman pushed one of the buttons, and the hand made a high-pitched sound.

"There's an easy or a hard way to do this. You decide," she said, pointing the hand at William. "Either you come willingly, or . . ."

William froze. What was she doing? Was that hand some kind of weapon?

"Defragging is quite painful," she said.

"Defragging?" William backed up. He was not going to let this woman capture him.

"Oh," the woman said. "It only rips your atoms apart and turns you into a heap of dust. I can reassemble you again later. . . ."

The high-pitched sound grew louder. Before he knew it, William had thrown himself to the side as a beam shot out from the woman's hand. The beam hit a streetlight behind him. William landed on his back in the middle of the street. He jolted back up and, to his horror, saw that the light was gone. It was like it had never been there at all.

The woman opened a small lid in her mechanical hand and tilted it to the side, and metal dust poured onto the pavement.

"I need you to solve something I have acquired. It won't take long. Not for a boy of your . . . abilities."

William got to his feet and started running in the opposite direction. But he had seen how fast the woman could move and knew that he wouldn't be able to outrun her. Still, he kept going.

As he ran, William noticed a black car coming up the street toward him.

He leaped over the nearest fence and ducked down. He heard the car come to a halt on the other side.

He got up and was about to escape farther into the garden, when he heard a familiar voice.

"William, get in."

William turned and gasped as Tobias Wenton, his grandfather, appeared in the car window. He waved at him.

William looked back at the spot where the woman had been, but she was gone.

He was about to jump into the car when he stopped. Abraham Talley had once tricked him by shape-shifting into his grandfather.

It seemed like his grandfather knew what he was thinking and knocked on the window in front of him. The window lowered, and one of the bearded chauffeurs peered out at him. There was something about the two chauffeurs that made William uncomfortable, but they had saved him several times already. They looked completely human, but he knew they were highly advanced androids.

William jumped into the car, which accelerated the minute the door closed behind him.

William sat up in his seat and looked out the back window. The strange woman was gone.

"Who was that you were talking to?" Tobias asked.

"I don't know," William said. "Some woman. She shot at me."

"What?" his grandfather said. He seemed surprised.

William nodded.

"Are you okay?"

"I think so," William said, and looked down at his body.

"She shot at you?" his grandfather asked. "With what?"

"She had a funny hand," William said. "Mechanical. It fired rays that made stuff disappear."

The color in Tobias's face drained away, and he turned to stare out the window. William shifted in his seat uncomfortably.

"Do you know who she is?" William asked.

"Did she say anything to you?" his grandfather asked.

"She wanted me to go with her," William said. It wasn't until now that he felt his body shaking from all the adrenaline. He took a deep breath and tried to relax.

Finally, his grandfather turned toward him.

"Good thing we came when we did, then," he said, and forced a smile.

"Do you know who she is?" William asked again.

"No," his grandfather said, and paused. "Not yet . . ."

William got the feeling his grandfather was holding out on something.

"I saw what happened on TV yesterday," his grandfather said. It seemed like he wanted to change the subject.

It felt like a big rock hit William in the gut. He had been foolish to think his grandfather might not have found out about his seizures. Of course he had, right along with the rest of Norway. William hoped it wouldn't prevent him from going back to the Institute.

"I don't know what happened. It was as if . . ."

"As if you lost control of your body?" his grandfather asked.

"Yes." William nodded and looked down at his hands. "Do you know what could have caused it?"

"We have to run some tests on you to find out." His grandfather paused a little. "Are you ready to come back to the Institute?" he asked, tousling William's hair.

"Yes," William said, and nodded.

"Great." Grandfather smiled. "I thought you would be. We'll message your parents on the way so they know where you're going."

His grandfather cast a quick glance out the rear window, then turned and knocked on the glass between them and the drivers.

William tipped back in the seat as the car accelerated.

# 5

**A few hours later William arrived at the Institute for Post-**Human Research. They had driven to a secret airfield not far from his home in Norway, where a high-tech plane had collected both them and the car.

And now the car came to a halt outside the Institute's gates in England.

His grandfather pointed at two guard-bots in front of the gates. "After Abraham Talley was placed in the basement, we had to raise the security level."

One of the guard-bots wheeled toward them and stopped next to the car. They looked like fire hydrants on wheels. They had two arms and one large eye at the top of their heads, which could rotate 360 degrees like an owl. At the Institute, they were known for their stubborn single-mindedness and not their people skills.

Grandfather lowered the electric window and peered out.

"Identification scan." The guard-bot raised something that looked like an advanced clothing iron.

"Certainly," William's grandfather said, and stuck his head out the window.

The guard-bot placed the scanner to Tobias's forehead and pressed a button. The scanner hummed for a bit, and a lamp on top of it blinked red a couple of times before it turned green.

"Tobias Wenton. Clear," the guard-bot said.

"Your turn." Grandfather motioned for William to do the same. "It scans your brain, which is the most accurate form of identification."

After William had been cleared, the car continued through the gates. A long, gravel drive led to the Institute building. A large lawn stretched out on both sides of the road. William didn't see any people, but several guard-bots patrolled the area.

"Where are all the people?" William asked.

"We've had to send a big majority home," Grandfather said. "The Institute is more like a high-security prison now than an advanced research facility."

"All because of Abraham?" William asked.

"More or less." Tobias seemed far from pleased.

The car stopped in front of the main doors. William looked up at the stone building looming above them. Even if it had been only a little more than four months, it felt like forever since he'd last been here.

William opened the door and almost jumped out. He was excited to be back. Then he felt his grandfather's hand on his arm. "William," he said. "I won't be coming with you."

"What?" William asked.

"I have to get going," his grandfather continued.

"But you're coming back," William said. "Soon?"

"There's some urgent business I have to take care of."

"Urgent?" William said.

His grandfather paused, looking at William.

"There's been a minor incident here at the Institute. . . . Something's gone missing, and I'm going to try to get it back."

"What's gone missing?" William asked.

"Nothing you need to worry about," Tobias said. "You have your own problems to sort out."

William couldn't believe it. He had been looking forward for so long to spending time with his grandfather. And now that he had finally come back to the Institute, his grandfather was leaving again?

"I'm sorry," his grandfather said gently. "There's so much

happening right now. I wish I could stay here and explain. But Benjamin Slapperton will take good care of you. He would like to test you right away. We want to find out what's up with you sooner rather than later. And after that I've asked him and Fritz Goffman to explain more."

William sat back in his seat. He tried to puzzle everything out. His seizures . . . the strange woman who had attacked him . . . the heightened security at the Institute . . . his grandfather's haste to get back to his mission . . . Somehow he felt that all this was connected.

"That woman," William began, "the one outside school. How does she fit in to all this?"

"I don't know yet. We'll let you know as soon as we find out." Tobias pointed at something behind William. "There he is now."

William turned and saw Benjamin Slapperton coming out the large doors. He seemed nervous, his eyes scanning the surroundings.

"You'd better get a move on," his grandfather said.

Benjamin waved at William and disappeared back inside.

William exited the car and closed the door behind him. The vehicle shot forward and left down the same road they had come up. William turned and hurried up the stairs.

William stepped inside a large hall. Benjamin was waiting next to something that looked like a hovering golf cart.

"Finally," he said, jumping into the driver's seat.

The cart sat on top of a black rubber cushion, and there was a large fan secured behind the seats.

"We don't have much time," Benjamin said, patting the seat beside him. He pushed a button on the dashboard, and the fan whirred to life.

William sat next to Benjamin, and they zoomed down the hallway. The air cushion occasionally bumped into the walls, so William quickly fastened his seat belt before looking up at Benjamin. He was happy to see his old teacher again. Benjamin's dark hair fluttered in the airstream from the fan behind them while the vibrations caused his glasses to bounce up and down on his nose. In spite of the strap holding him in, William almost fell off as Slapperton turned the steering wheel and they swerved sideways into a new corridor. The cart hit the wall and continued onward even faster. William held on to the seat with both hands.

"Why are we in such a hurry?" he said over the noise from the fan.

"Look around." Benjamin pointed with one hand. "The Institute isn't the same."

"I know," William said. "Because of Abraham."

"Exactly," Benjamin said. "Nothing can be done around here anymore. I only leave my lab when it's absolutely necessary."

"But why all the security?" William asked. "He's frozen. It's not like he's gonna get up and leave."

"This is Abraham Talley we're talking about," Benjamin said. "We can't be too careful. Besides, we don't know if he has any more followers out there. So the security is more about keeping anyone from getting in rather than him getting out."

"People getting in?" William asked. "To rescue him?"

"It's just a precaution really," Benjamin said. "We think all the ones who used to help him are long dead. One of the downsides of being semi-immortal like he is."

Benjamin hit the brakes so hard that William was flung forward in his seat. "But it's a huge nuisance to those of us here at the Institute who are trying to get some serious work done." He gestured at two guard-bots standing in front of a barrier blocking the hallway. One of the guard-bots rolled up to their cart.

"We went through all this four minutes ago." Benjamin seemed irritated.

The guard-bot didn't respond and held up the same kind of scanner the robots by the gates had used.

After they both passed the scan, the guard-bot pressed a button on the wall. The gate swung up and slammed back with a metallic clank.

Benjamin stepped on the gas, and the hovercart moved forward again.

"No one's allowed to travel in the hallways without clearance. And anyone under the age of eighteen needs to be accompanied," Benjamin said.

"But then how am I supposed to get around?" William asked.

"We'd prefer it if you didn't," Benjamin said, and turned the wheel again.

They swerved around a corner and kept going down another long corridor. The air cushion grazed a red robot that looked like a large soda can on wheels. It had one large eye that traveled along the rim at the top.

"But if you must get to somewhere alone," Benjamin said, pointing at the robot they'd almost run over, "you use one of those."

"Look where you're going," the robot shouted after them.

"That was a porter-bot. They're all over the Institute. You hail one and it will come, like grabbing a cab. Or you can order one from your room when you want to go out. Your door will arrange it."

They passed a couple of guard-bots carrying laserlike guns. The robots stopped and looked at William as they passed.

"What are those weapons?" William asked.

"Passivators," Benjamin said. "Nasty things. They shoot out rays that make the atoms in your body unstable. We call it jelly technology for lack of a more sophisticated word. Works on machines, too."

"What happens if you get shot with one?" William asked.

"Your body becomes wobbly like jelly," Benjamin said, and shuddered. "Stay away from them."

"Has it been like this ever since Abraham arrived?" William asked.

"Yes," Benjamin said. "Most of the candidates have gone."

"What about Iscia?" William asked. He'd been looking forward to seeing her, but now he was afraid that she had left too.

"She's one of the few still here," Benjamin said. "She's a field assistant now."

She was at the Institute! William felt a surge of relief. He couldn't wait to see her again.

"What's a field assistant?" William asked.

"She's no longer a candidate. She has real duties now." Benjamin turned the wheel, and they swerved into another hallway. "Here we are," he announced as the air cushion crashed into the wall next to a metal door.

William read the sign on the door: ULTRASONIC LAB.

Benjamin hopped out of the hovercart and glanced from side to side like a scared mouse. He entered a code on the control panel next to the door, which emitted a brief blip.

"In we go," he said, opening the door and waving William in. "This is where the magic happens."

**6**

**Inside the lab Benjamin seemed to relax a little more. But**
not before he'd secured all eight of the locks on the door
and bolted it with an iron bar.

Finally, he turned to William and looked at him properly for the first time.

"You've changed," he said. "Gotten taller . . . more than
an inch. How long has it been since you were here? Three
months?"

"Four months and thirteen days," William said. He'd
counted every single day. "I thought I'd be able to come
back sooner."

"I understand. But the circumstances are a little unusual
right now. We didn't want to bring you back until it was
necessary."

"And now it is?" William asked.

"You could put it that way, yes," Benjamin said. "We have been paying attention."

"Paying attention to what?" William asked.

"To you," Benjamin said.

"Why?" The thought of someone spying on him didn't sit well.

"In case of things like your seizures." Benjamin fiddled with a device next to him. "We wanted to keep track of the luridium in your body." He watched William for a moment before clapping his hands. "I want to show you something. Follow me!"

Benjamin proceeded farther into the lab amid all the instruments. William followed him over to a steel-framed glass tank standing on a table. William stopped beside Benjamin and looked at what was behind the thick glass.

"Do you see what that is?" Benjamin asked.

"Yes," William responded with a nod. "A cockroach."

There, inside the tank, sat an average-size cockroach. It was waving its antennae around, and it moved a little closer to the glass, as if it realized they were there. It seemed to be looking right at them.

"We found it in the bunker under London," Benjamin said. "After the water from the Thames flooded the bunker, we had to use submarines to explore the area. We found a large network of passageways down there."

William shuddered, remembering what had happened in the bunker in London. It had only been a little over four months ago, but it felt like forever. He'd tried not to think about it too much. But now it all came back to him. The dark, endless tunnels. The big door that only opened with the right code. The cavernous hall with the submarines and military vehicles. And the cryogenic storage containers where he'd found Abraham Talley. The same Abraham Talley who was now lying frozen solid down in the Institute's basement.

"We found the cockroach in one of the air pockets," Benjamin said. "As a matter of course we brought it back here to study it, the way we do with everything we find down there, and . . ." He stopped and stood there watching the cockroach.

"And?" William prompted.

"In a way, you and that cockroach are in the same boat," Benjamin said.

"How so?" William asked.

"Because of what you have inside you."

William stared at Benjamin. "You mean luridium?"

"It doesn't have much inside it, but then it's not that big, either."

Benjamin looked at William and then back at the cockroach.

"If you were to touch it, the luridium inside of you, being a larger amount, would pull the luridium out of the cockroach . . . and into you."

"Like Abraham tried to do to me in London," William added.

"Correct," Benjamin said. "And the funny thing is that the roach has exactly enough luridium inside of it to make you fifty-fifty . . . exactly half-human, half-machine."

William looked at the little insect.

"What would happen to me then?" William asked, intrigued.

"Your abilities would increase," Benjamin said. "But at a great risk."

"What risk?"

"Being fifty-fifty . . . you might tip over . . . and become more machine than human."

"Or more human?"

"Yes. Depending on which side is predominant."

"Is that what happened to Abraham Talley?" William asked. "He tipped over?"

"That's right. He lost the human in him completely."

William looked at the cockroach. Was it really possible to become a machine? Up until now, William had thought of the luridium inside his body as a blessing. After his crushing spinal injury, it did, after all, keep him alive. But the thought that the same thing that was saving him could also cause him to lose his human qualities was devastating. What was the difference between that and dying? It felt like he had an enemy inside him. An enemy he could never get rid of. Could the seizures be the beginning of the end?

He had to find out more.

"How did it get the luridium?" William asked, peering at the cockroach.

Benjamin shrugged. "I don't know. Must have stumbled over it somewhere."

"But I thought luridium was very rare," William said.

"It is." Benjamin watched the cockroach, which had now come nearer to the thick glass.

"Why are you keeping it locked up like that?" William asked. He leaned a little closer to see better.

"It was a fantastic opportunity to study and do laboratory tests on a living creature with luridium in it." Benjamin paused for a bit. "And it went great right up until yesterday."

"What happened then?" William asked.

"I'm sure you remember, right?" Benjamin said.

William thought it over. Then it hit him.

"You mean my attack . . . during the TV show?"

"Exactly," Benjamin said. "You both have luridium inside you, and you both had attacks at the same time." He was talking faster now. "The cockroach was acting strange. It started trembling. And its body temperature plummeted."

He looked at William to see how he would react.

"So . . . ," Benjamin started, but stopped, as if he was having trouble figuring out what he wanted to say.

"What?" William asked. He felt like they were talking more about him than the cockroach now.

"It ruined half my lab," Benjamin said. "Demolished it. Do you see that over there?" He pointed to some deep grooves in the concrete wall.

William nodded.

"It did that, tried to eat its way through the wall." Benjamin shuddered. "Looked like it was trying to get somewhere."

"If we both had attacks," William said, "it must have something to do with the luridium."

"Yes," Benjamin said. "And I think I know what caused it."

William looked at Benjamin. "You do?"

"Yes." Benjamin nodded. "But I don't know where it came from yet."

"What was it, then?" William gasped.

"Sound waves," Benjamin said. His voice was trembling with excitement now. "Watch this."

Benjamin pushed a couple of buttons on a control panel next to the tank. The cockroach started vibrating and then flew at them, crashing into the glass.

William backed away and stopped. He stood there watching the cockroach thump its head into the pane of glass. Then it did a backward somersault and hit the wall before racing around in a circle. Now and then it crashed into the walls in what looked like an attempt to bust its way out.

Benjamin pushed the button again, and the vibrations stopped. The cockroach lay lifeless for a few seconds before it got back up onto its legs. It shook itself off a little and then seemed to be fine again.

"What did you do?" William said without taking his eyes off the cockroach.

"High-frequency sound waves," Benjamin said. "I have re-created the frequency of the sound waves that triggered your attack."

"But why didn't anything happen to me this time?" William asked.

"Reinforced soundproof glass," Benjamin replied, and rapped on the glass. Then he turned to William. "Okay, now it's your turn."

"My turn?" William said.

**7**

**"I hope you're okay with this,"** Benjamin said, pointing to a chair in the middle of the room. "I have to run some experiments before I know if I can help you or not."

William stared at the strange-looking contraption.

It looked like a dentist's chair surrounded by various weird instruments. William walked over to it and stopped. He didn't want to sit in it. He'd never been a big fan of dentists. And after he saw what had happened to the cockroach, he wasn't a fan of sound waves, either. He glanced up at some type of pointy laser cannon mounted on the ceiling over the chair.

"What's that?" he asked.

"Relax," Benjamin said with a smile. "It's not as dangerous as it looks. I call it an audio-sonic regulator."

"But what does it do?" William asked.

"I'm going to send high-frequency sound waves into you," Benjamin said, as if this were obvious, and then started tinkering with the cannon.

"Like the cockroach?"

Benjamin nodded and smiled apologetically.

"I watched you on TV." Benjamin patted William on the back. "First, I want you to forget everything that happened there. That Vektor guy is a big show-off. He has nothing on you."

William smiled and relaxed a little.

"When I got back to my lab after the show," Benjamin said, pointing at a large box in a corner, "I noticed that the audiometer over there had short-circuited."

"What's an audiometer?" William asked.

"It's like a seismometer, which is used to register earthquakes," Benjamin said. "Only the audiometer measures sound waves that are inaudible to the human ear." Benjamin hesitated and stared at the audiometer for a little while. "The audiometer works 24/7, constantly monitoring the airwaves. During the TV show, it registered sound frequencies so high the audiometer fried. I don't know where the waves are coming from, but I calculated the frequency that caused it and programmed it into the cannon."

William looked at the cannon above the chair.

"So, you're going to make me have another attack with

that cannon?" William asked. He already knew Benjamin's answer, and he didn't like it.

Benjamin seemed to understand that this scared him. He smiled and patted William on the back.

"William, this attack . . ." The smile vanished from Benjamin's face. "It's not only painful for you. When you lose control of your body and your mind . . . then you become a threat not only to yourself but to everyone around you. You saw what happened to the cockroach."

William gulped.

Could he be dangerous? Hurt someone?

William went and sat in the strange chair. He glanced up at the cannon, which pointed right at him. Benjamin pressed a few buttons on a control panel, and it started humming.

"Could you place your arms there?" he asked, pointing to the armrests on either side. "I have to strap you in. . . . It's for your own safety." Benjamin appeared to force himself to smile.

"It'll be okay. I've done this many times before on the cockroach, and it's been completely fine. I'll start out gently and then increase the waves, little by little."

Benjamin pushed a button on the side of the chair, and the seat back started vibrating.

"Are you ready?"

William nodded. "I'm ready."

Benjamin took out a pair of safety headphones and placed them on William's head. He then took cover behind a screen that looked like the kind used when taking X-rays. He put on a huge helmet and a heavy-looking jacket with a badge that read LEAD PROTECTIVE WEAR.

*Not dangerous?* William thought. *Nothing to worry about?* It looked like Benjamin was about to detonate a nuclear bomb.

Slapperton pulled a lever, and the sound cannon began to hum. William grabbed the armrests and squeezed his eyes closed.

At first he was only aware of the loud, humming sound from the cannon over him. Now he understood why he had to wear ear protection. Without it, this would make him deaf. Then he began to feel the vibrations traveling through his body in waves. It felt like he was disintegrating.

The noise soon moved into his head, and the vibrations spread down his spine. William opened his eyes and looked at Benjamin.

"What's happening?" he shouted.

But Benjamin was busy fiddling with the control panel and couldn't hear him.

William felt a stinging pain in his head. Then the high-pitched sound he had heard during his previous attacks. The pain increased until it felt like his head was going to explode.

He opened his mouth to yell to Benjamin, but he couldn't make a sound. It was as if he'd lost control of his own body.

A terrible cold spread all the way out to his hands, like the last times he'd suffered the attacks. A violent jolt traveled through him, and he shot out from the top of his head.

Everything around him was gone. And in its place was a bright white light.

It looked like snow. It felt like he was floating high up in the air, in the middle of a blizzard.

He spotted something far down below him.

An enormous mountain chain.

He thought he recognized it from pictures. Was it the Himalayas?

He plunged down toward the mountains at a tremendous speed. He was going to crash right into the tallest peak.

When he opened his eyes again, he was standing in a huge cave with gray stone walls.

A large metal ring hovered in the middle of the hall—the same golden ring he had seen during his other attacks.

It looked like a gigantic golden Hula-Hoop.

William spotted an object on the ground below the ring. It looked like a white coffin on wheels. There was something menacing about the oblong box. William felt as though he should know what it was, but he was certain that he'd never seen it before.

He felt himself starting to panic. And all he wanted was to get away.

Then it was like everything exploded in a white light again, and he was back in his chair.

William looked around. Benjamin's head popped up from behind the screen. He ripped off his protective gear and ran over to the chair.

"Sit still," he said, peering into William's ear with an otoscope. "Open wide." William opened his mouth, and Benjamin shined a small flashlight inside.

"Looks normal," he mumbled, and made a note on his notepad. "How do you feel?"

William thought for a moment. He felt shaken, shocked, and confused all at once. What had just happened? It was as if he'd traveled out of his body. Or were the mountains and the strange golden ring just something that his brain had made up?

"What happened?" William asked.

Benjamin was busy undoing the straps around his arms.

"You're the only one who knows, actually. If anything happened, it was inside your head," Benjamin said.

"I saw a bright light," William said. "And then I was way up in the air."

"Yes . . . ? Yes?" Benjamin exclaimed. "And?"

"I saw mountains."

"Mountains?" Benjamin said, straightening up.

He stared at William as if he didn't quite believe him. "What kind of mountains?"

"Big ones. Maybe the Himalayas," William replied.

Benjamin looked terrified. "The Himalayas? Are you sure?" he asked, his voice trembling.

"Don't know," William said. "Pretty sure . . ."

"Did you see anything else?" Benjamin leaned in closer.

"I saw a big room deep down inside the mountains. . . ."

"Go on!"

"And a kind of floating circle . . . like a huge golden ring. And a white box or coffin on wheels."

Benjamin stood there, staring at William and scratching his forehead.

"That's not good, is it?" William asked.

"No . . . it's not good," Benjamin said. "It's not good at all."

# 8

The hovercart came to a sudden halt as it bumped into the wall next to the door that led into William's room.

"We'll do some more, less painful tests tomorrow." Benjamin clutched the steering wheel and scanned the hallway with worried eyes.

"Okay," William said, and climbed out of the cart.

Although the ordeal had been an unpleasant one, he felt fine now. He was looking forward to seeing his room again.

"I have to make sure you get safely inside," Benjamin said, tapping his fingers on the steering wheel.

William turned the handle and pushed the door open.

"I'll pick you up tomorrow," Benjamin shouted as the large fan behind him hummed to life again. "And, William . . ."

"What?" William shouted back.

"It's important that you don't solve any codes while we're trying to figure out what's causing your attacks. Okay? We don't want anything to set off an attack accidentally."

William nodded and watched as the hovercart shot off down the hallway. He continued through the door and stopped, taking in the room.

Finally, he was back. But something was different.

The bed and desk had been bolted to the floor. Daylight seeped into the room through metal bars outside the little window. All the walls were covered with thick, dull steel plates. The room looked like a prison cell.

"Welcome, William," the door said as it closed with a click behind him.

"Door?" William said as he turned and looked.

"Would you like a cupcake?" the door asked.

A hatch opened next to the door, and a long arm shot out. It stopped right in front of William's face with a fresh cupcake on a plate, still warm from the oven.

William stared at it.

"Cool, huh?" the door said. "I got a new arm! Much more practical. Now I can finally bake."

But cupcakes were the furthest thing from William's mind right now. "What happened to my room?" he asked.

"Do you want the cupcake or not?" The mechanical arm extended even farther, like a telescope, shoving the cake in William's face.

"No thanks." William pushed the cupcake away.

"It's called the Isolator," the door said, sounding a little disappointed.

"The Isolator?" William said.

"Yes," the door said. "That's what they call it when a room is secured this way. You could explode a bomb in here without anyone hearing it."

"It looks like a holding cell," William said as his eyes scanned the room.

"You're free to come and go as you wish if you use a porter-bot," the door said. "Cupcake?"

"No thanks."

"I've really made an effort," the door said. "I thought you liked cupcakes."

"I do," William said. "But not now." He shivered as he walked over to the window and looked through the bars.

He could hardly believe what he saw.

A tall white fence extended all the way around the enormous grounds, almost as tall as the trees. Unmanned vehicles with cannons on their roofs patrolled along the wall. And there were tall watchtowers with enormous spotlights mounted on top.

"If you're thinking things are worse than the last time you were here, then you're wrong," the door said. "It's actually *much* worse. . . . That's why I've taken up pastries. To lighten things up. It's getting cold." The arm held up the cupcake.

"All of this because there's a frozen old man in the basement?" William tried to ignore the cupcake hovering in front of his face.

"Not any old man," the door said. "He has the potential for great destruction in him."

William fell silent. He looked at his hands. The door had hit a sore spot. The luridium—the very thing that made Abraham Talley so dangerous—was the same stuff William had inside him. He felt more like a freak than ever before.

"I'm sorry," the door said. "I didn't mean to . . ."

"That's okay," William said. "I'll take that cupcake now." He could use the sugar.

He took a bite. It was delicious.

"It was only a couple of days ago that the security was upped to level five," the door said.

"Really? I thought it was because of Abraham. What happened?" William asked with his mouth full of cake. It was clear that the door wanted to make things good by delivering some gossip.

"I'm not supposed to tell you," the door said.

"But you just did," William said, and swallowed.

"I know, but that was only to make you feel better."

"I would feel even better if you told me more," William said, and took another bite of the cupcake.

"When Abraham arrived here, the security level was raised to three. Then something happened in the Depository yesterday, and they raised it all the way to level five."

William walked over and looked right at the door.

"The Depository?" he said. "What's the Depository?"

"Never mind," the door said.

"What happened there?" William asked.

"Nothing," the door said.

William knew the door well enough to realize it had said something it shouldn't have.

"What happened in the Depository?" William asked again, and moved closer.

"Would you like another cupcake?" The hatch opened, and the mechanical arm shot out and held the pastry right in front of William's face. "This one has a hint of vanilla."

William pushed the arm away. "I *want* to know what happened in the Depository!"

The door stayed silent.

"Come on," William said. "I have to know. Something strange is going on, and I need to find out. It might be related to what's happening to me."

"All I can say is that something happened in the Depository for Impossible Archaeology . . . and after that they moved something from the Depository to one of the sonic labs in the basement. There's been a lot of activity down there. I'm sorry, but I can't tell you anything more. If they find out, they'll give me refrigerator duty for the rest of my life."

William knew that he wouldn't get any more information from the door, not now anyway. But he had enough to work with. He was sure about one thing: Something strange was going on at the Institute.

He needed to find out what it was, and the basement seemed a good place to start.

"I need some fresh air," William said. "Could you order me one of those porter-bots?"

"Now?" the door said. There was hesitation in its voice.

"Yes, now!" William said.

The door was silent for a little bit.

"It's a little late," the door said. "But maybe I can get hold of one . . . if you'll try another cupcake."

# 9

**Five minutes later William walked briskly down the hallway**
outside his room. He took a bite of his second cupcake. The
taste of vanilla flooded his mouth. The door really did know
his cupcakes.

A porter-bot wheeled in front of him. William had
told the porter-bot that he had dropped something outside
Benjamin's laboratory. And now they were headed downstairs to find it. William didn't like lying, not even to a robot.
But he felt that, in this case, the end justified the means. He
had to find out what was going on at the Institute.

"We need to hurry," the robot said, turning a corner and
speeding up. "I'm picking someone else up in four minutes
and thirty-eight seconds. I'm on my third triple shift this

week. And I'm running low on oil and electrolytes. No time to recharge."

William jogged to catch up with the stressed-out bot.

"I'm sure I can find my own way down there," William said.

"Anyone under eighteen is forbidden from moving around the Institute alone." The porter-bot accelerated even more.

"But isn't that a precaution? There's no real danger around here?"

William knew that there was a good reason for the heightened security. But he was fishing to see what the porter-bot knew. Sometimes the robots blurted out stuff they weren't supposed to say.

"Danger?" the porter-bot said. "Right now there's more danger than ever. Only two days ago they raised the security level by two whole points. Do you think they would have done that if there was no danger? It's so bad now that some of the porter-bots refuse to work alone. You've probably seen them roaming around in groups. Following each other."

"Two days ago?" William said. "I thought it was raised when they brought Abraham here, and that was more than four months ago."

"When Abraham came, they raised the security level to three," the porter-bot said. "What I'm trying to tell you is that two days ago it was raised again, to level five."

"Why?" William asked. He was running now to keep up with the robot.

"Don't know," the porter-bot said. "Our orders are to be on the lookout for things out of the ordinary."

"What kinds of things?" William said.

"Someone who's not supposed to be here," the porter-bot said, and sped up.

"Someone?" William asked. "You mean a person?"

"Shoot. Now we have even less time. We need to take a shortcut." The robot seemed to have tired of the security conversation. The porter-bot turned into a narrower hallway and headed for the stairs at the other end. William ran after it.

"But . . . ," William protested. So far everything the robot had said backed up what the door had told him, but he wanted to know more. This robot clearly knew a lot and had a loose robot tongue as well.

"I don't usually go this way. But it's thirty-eight seconds faster than the other route," said the porter-bot. It continued over the edge of the stairs and bumped down the steps.

William stopped and watched the porter-bot clank downward like an out-of-control garbage can. Finally, it landed on the floor at the bottom of the stairs and continued.

"Hurry up," the robot said as it whizzed off down the hallway.

William grabbed the handrail and jumped down the stairs, three steps at a time. He knew that going down there was probably a very bad idea. But his need to know was stronger than his fear right now.

The porter-bot was waiting for him in front of an elevator door at the other end of the hallway.

"Come on," it said, and waved. "We have to get going!"

The robot raised its hand up to a sensor on the wall next to the door.

"Authorized," the door said, and opened.

The robot continued into the elevator. William followed. The door closed.

"Ground level Two A," the porter-bot said.

"Two A coming up," the elevator said, and, with a nudge, started its descent.

William looked at the porter-bot's hand.

"Do you have access to the whole Institute?" he asked.

"More or less," the robot said. "Why?" The robot eyed William suspiciously.

"Just making conversation," William said.

William thought back to the orbs the Institute had given all the candidates the first time he had come here. The orbs had to be solved, and for every new level, the orb gave them access to new parts of the Institute.

"There are places I can't go," said the robot. "Restricted areas because of heightened security levels."

"Okay," William said.

"Like Two B . . . ," the robot blurted, but stopped itself.

"Two B?" William said, looking at the robot. "What's at Two B?"

"Nothing," the robot said. "It's extremely restricted!"

"Level Two A," the elevator said, followed by a soft ding, and the doors opened.

"Come on." The porter-bot shot out of the elevator.

William didn't move. It was on a whim, but he knew that he had to lose the porter-bot if he was to do some exploring on his own. And now was his chance. He watched as the porter-bot continued down the hallway. It was in such a hurry that it didn't even notice that William was still inside the elevator.

"Doors closing," the elevator said.

William still didn't move.

The doors shut in front of him.

"Level Two B," William said.

"Level Two B, coming up," the elevator said.

When the elevator doors opened again, William peered into the hallway outside. It looked the same as the one he had just left, only much darker.

"Doors closing," the elevator said.

William hesitated. He knew that if he left the elevator he would have a hard time getting in again since he had no form of authorization.

The doors started closing, and he jumped out.

He stood and watched the doors close, then turned and

looked at the dark hallway in front of him. It ended in an L junction about twenty yards farther down. There was a sign on the wall. It said HIGHLY RESTRICTED. KEEP OUT!

He didn't particularly want to be down here any longer than necessary. Not after the porter-bot had said that everyone was supposed to be on the lookout for someone who didn't belong. William caught himself wishing that Iscia were here with him. He strode down the hallway, and the sound of his footsteps echoed.

He slowed as he got closer to the corner at the end of the hallway; then he stopped and listened.

Nothing.

He snuck up and peaked around the corner.

A sign on the wall read FORBIDDEN. TURN AROUND (BESIDES, THERE'S NOTHING OF INTEREST HERE)!

There were also two cameras. One in each corner. Whoever was watching would have already spotted him, and that meant that guard-bots would be on their way. He didn't have much time. Whatever was down there, the Institute didn't want anyone getting too close.

But William knew that he had already passed the point of no return. If he wanted to get some answers, any answers, he had to move fast. See how far he could get before he was stopped. William's gaze landed on something that looked like an advanced control panel on the wall. It was his only chance of getting in. He would need to hack his way into the system using the panel. He leaned in for a closer look.

He took a deep breath and focused. He immediately felt the vibrations starting in his stomach. His only concern now was being apprehended by a bunch of guard-bots with passivators.

William focused his attention on the digits and letters on the control panel. He felt the vibrations move up his spine and out into his arms and fingers. Then, as it always did, everything around him seemed to vanish, and all he could see was the control panel.

One digit after another started lighting up. They blinked like disco lights. At first randomly, but then a pattern emerged. William knew that the lights were only in his head and that the luridium in his body was helping his brain find the solution. Still, his fingers started working, pressing the buttons quickly.

The flashing lights blinked so fast now, William had a hard time keeping up. This code was a tough one.

Finally, his fingers stopped and the lights disappeared.

He straightened up, rubbing his sore hands as he looked at the panel. Had he made it?

The control panel flashed a couple of times before it gave a quick beep, and the heavy metal doors opened.

William looked back; he was still alone in the hallway. He slipped inside, and the door closed behind him.

# 10

**William now stood in some kind of laboratory.**

The walls and ceiling were covered with golden metal. It looked like a space station. A symphony of bleeps and hums came at him from rows of sophisticated equipment along the walls.

In the middle of the room were two curtains on wheels, like the ones used around beds in hospitals, only much larger.

A white cannon hung from the ceiling. It looked like the same thing Benjamin had used on William during his test.

William stood motionless for a while, debating whether he should leave or continue. He had come this far; he had to investigate further.

William started toward the curtain walls. And as he came closer, he heard a noise. At first, the cacophony of computer noises had drowned it out. But now he heard it. *Puff . . . puff . . . puff . . .* over and over. It sounded like a small locomotive.

William had to fight the urge to turn and run. It hit him that getting that close to the cannon might trigger a seizure, but still he kept going.

He stopped in front of the curtains and listened to the rhythmic sound coming from the other side: *Puff . . . puff . . . puff . . .*

He might as well get it over with. William grabbed one of the curtains and pulled it aside.

Nothing could have prepared him for what he saw.

On the floor behind the curtain stood a large square steel slab. Sticking out of it was an elderly man with gray hair and a beard. He was wearing a suit jacket, but everything below his waist was trapped inside the slab, which seemed to have melted and then trapped him like a bug in amber. But no one could survive being dipped into burning hot molten steel, could they?

The man's eyes were closed, and he had an oxygen mask over his nose and mouth. A tube ran to a breathing machine. The machine went *puff . . . puff . . . puff . . .* as it pumped air into the man's lungs.

William stared at the man with a mix of curiosity and dread.

"Hello?" he said.

But the man didn't react.

William moved even closer. The man had a name tag on his jacket lapel: PONTUS DIPPEL, DEPOSITORY FOR IMPOS-SIBLE ARCHAEOLOGY.

William's door had said that something had been moved from the Depository. Was this the mysterious thing the door had been talking about?

William studied the old man's wrinkled face, then leaned forward and touched his hand. It was warm. William glanced up at the big white cannon pointing straight down at them. What were they planning on doing to the old man with that cannon?

The man's body jerked like he'd been jolted by electricity. His eyes flew open, and he screamed at the top of his lungs, "SHE'S COMING . . . SHE'S COMING!"

William backed away. He stood there staring in terror at the old man, who twisted and turned, trying to get free.

"SHE'S COMING!" the old man shouted again.

William wanted to help, but he didn't have a clue what he should do.

"Please, calm down," he said urgently.

Then the old man's eyes closed again, and his head slumped forward.

William heard an electric hum behind him.

He turned and saw the door opening and three guard-bots rushing toward him. His little excursion was about to end.

One of the guard-bots raised its passivator. And before William had time to react, a beam shot out and hit him. He felt his whole body go limp, and he fell to the floor like a wet towel.

# 11

**The two guard-bots stopped in front of a white door.**

They carried William between them on a stretcher. His body was still completely wobbly, like all his bones had turned to jelly. And he couldn't move a muscle. Only his eyes. His hands and feet had started to tingle. And he suspected that crazy wobble technology was wearing off. He tried to see where they were, but the anonymous white walls revealed nothing.

There was a soft hum as the door in front of them opened, and the guard-bots continued into the room on the other side.

The two robots placed William in a large leather chair. He had enough control over his body now to stay upright.

Large bookshelves loomed over him on all sides. There

was a mahogany desk in front of him. As his brain came back to life, William started to recognize the office. He had been here before.

The sun was low in the sky and twinkled in through a picture window. William could see the silhouette of a tall man with a cane standing by the window with his back to him.

Finally, the man turned to face him.

"You don't waste much time, do you, William?" the man said.

William recognized the voice right away.

"How do you feel?" the man said.

"A little shaky," William said, watching as Fritz Goffman approached him.

Goffman was the head of the Institute. He was also one of the people who had saved William from Abraham Talley four months earlier. It was thanks to Goffman that he was still alive. If it hadn't been for him, Abraham would have succeeded in sucking all the luridium out of his body.

"It's completely normal to feel a little shaky after passivization," Goffman said, coming to a halt. His long arms hung down beside his skinny body, and the sun glistened off his black suit.

Goffman pulled up his sleeve and glanced at the large watch that he wore on one of his sinewy wrists. The gesture seemed like a habit.

"The Institute owes you a debt of gratitude, William." Goffman cleared his throat. "But that doesn't mean you can walk around the building and go wherever you want. Particularly not under these circumstances."

It was obvious that Goffman was not particularly pleased.

"The porter-bot you ditched was so distraught that it had lost you," Goffman continued, "it had a nervous breakdown and was rushed down to maintenance. It's still traumatized. It's talking about reschooling."

William felt bad. He hadn't meant for the porter-bot to get in trouble.

"Are you thirsty?" Goffman asked, nodding at something behind William.

William turned around and spotted the two redheaded chauffeurs. One of them walked over to a small table with drinks and handed William a glass containing an orange liquid.

"Drink it," Goffman said. "It'll make you feel better."

William eyed the orange beverage.

"Relax. It's Mars juice," Goffman said. "A new kind. It'll give you your strength back."

William took a swig of the Mars juice, which had turned blue in a flash. It tasted heavenly. It sort of changed flavors while it was in his mouth. It went from orange to something like strawberry, and after that vanilla. William swallowed. He could feel the liquid go down his throat, and a warm sensation spread throughout his body. He sat up and looked at his hands. Moved his fingers. Stretched his legs. He had full control of his body again. He made a mental note to stay away from passivators in the future.

He looked up at Goffman.

"There was a man down there," William said, handing the glass back. "He was stuck in some kind of metal slab."

A serious expression came over Goffman's face. He cleared his throat again and tightened his grip on his cane, fumbling a little.

"A man . . . in a metal slab?" Goffman said. "Inside the room where the guard-bots found you?"

"Yes!" William said. "He was about my grandfather's age, and he was stuck in this block like it had melted under him."

William swallowed. He knew it sounded insane. But then again, Goffman had to know about the man already. And William had to find out how he'd ended up like that.

"William . . . ," began Goffman, leaning against the large desk. "I spoke with Benjamin Slapperton today about how your tests went. . . ."

William sat up in the chair. "What does that have to do with this?" William asked.

"He said that you . . . saw something when he was testing you," Goffman said. "That you hallucinated."

"Yes . . . ?" William said. "But that had nothing to do

with what I saw down there. There really was a man, and he really was stuck. . . ."

Goffman gave William a look. Like he felt sorry for him. William sat back in the chair again.

"Would you like to know what I think?" Goffman asked.

William nodded his head. Of course he wanted to know what Goffman thought.

"I think what you experienced in the basement was some kind of side effect from the experiment done in Benjamin's lab."

"But there was a man . . . ," William began.

"Listen to me, William. . . . There was no man down there," Goffman said.

"What do you mean?" William said. "I know what I saw."

"The security-bots found you in one of the empty sonic laboratories," Goffman said. He cleared his throat. "The robots thought you were . . . an intruder and had to passivize you."

William could hardly believe what he was hearing.

"What do you mean? Are you saying that I was hallucinating down there?"

Goffman sat watching William for what felt like forever.

"I suppose it's a disappointment to come back when everything is like this?" Goffman finally said.

William looked at the floor, feeling let down. He couldn't understand why Goffman didn't believe him.

"None of us is enjoying it either," Goffman said. "But this is how it has to be right now."

William looked up at him again. He felt a rush of frustration surging through him.

"What's wrong with me?" he asked, his voice trembling. "I want to know what's wrong with me."

Goffman nodded to the two chauffeurs, who turned and walked out of the room. Then he moved around behind his enormous desk and sat down in his chair. He rested his cane against the desk and took off his eyeglasses. He cleaned them on the lapel of his jacket and put them back on.

"I want the same thing as you, William." Goffman clasped his hands and leaned toward him. "And that's why I have Benjamin running the tests on you. To find out exactly what causes your attacks. Meanwhile, you take it easy until we find out."

"What about my grandfather?" William asked. "Why did he leave me here like this? What was so important that he had to leave right away, without even knowing what was wrong with me?"

"Tobias would have stayed if he could," Goffman said, his hands tightening until his knuckles turned white. "But there are important matters he had to take care of."

. "Something to do with the woman who attacked me outside school?" William asked, and frowned at Goffman.

It looked like Goffman didn't like the question. He got to his feet and walked over to the large window again.

"I don't want you to worry about people attacking you," Goffman said. "You're safe here."

"But what did she want?" William said. He didn't like the way everyone seemed to avoid giving him any straight answers.

"We're looking into it," Goffman said, and turned toward William.

"These are difficult times," he said. "So much has happened. The Institute hasn't been the same since Abraham was moved here. I don't know what did it. The thought of him lying down there in the basement made people nervous. Maybe he has some kind of negative energy that works even when he's in cold storage. But something happened the same day he arrived here. It was as if a veil of negativity and fear settled over the Institute."

Goffman swallowed. "I'm beginning to wonder if the Institute is ever going to be the same again," he added.

They sat in silence for a while. William studied Goffman's face for anything revealing. But like all the adults around here, he was trained in keeping secrets. And he was very good at it.

"There's one other thing," Goffman said. "It's very

important that you don't solve any codes. Not before Benjamin has found the reason for your attacks."

William nodded. This was the second time since he arrived that someone had told him not to solve codes, and he didn't like it.

As they sat there looking at each other, William knew one thing. He had to find out more about the old man in the basement *and* the strange woman who had attacked him. Somehow, he had a feeling that these things were related to whatever was causing his attacks.

# 12

**When the meeting with Goffman was over, two porter-bots** collected William.

Their orders were to take him directly back to his room.

Having two porter-bots guarding him seemed a little over the top, William thought. But Goffman didn't want to take any chances with him after his excursion to the basement. And now he was walking as fast as he could down the hallway, one porter-bot on each side. William hated the thought of having to be cooped up in that room again. It felt like a prison.

William's legs were still a little wobbly after the passivization, and he had a hard time keeping up with the porter-bots.

"Could we make a short pit stop?" William said.

"No," one of the porter-bots said. "We're supposed to bring you directly to your room."

"There's someone I need to talk to." William had to get hold of Iscia. She could help him find out more about the old man in the floor.

"Who?" the other porter-bot said.

"Iscia," William said. "She's one of the field assistants. I know where her room is."

"Forget it," the porter-bot said. "We have to bring you to your room."

For a moment William considered giving the robots the slip, but then thought better of it. He'd been in enough trouble for today. Besides, he didn't want to be passivized again.

"Here we are," one of the porter-bots said as they stopped outside his room.

The door opened, and William walked inside. He turned and looked at the two porter-bots still standing outside in the hallway. They wouldn't leave until he was safely inside.

"Welcome," the door said after it closed.

"Thanks." William looked at the door. "I need to get hold of someone. Can you help me?"

"Haven't you been in enough trouble already?" the door said.

"I can't even talk to any of my friends here at the Institute?" William said. "What is this, a prison?"

"I've got pastries on the way," the door said. "You hungry?"

"No thank you," William said, and took a step closer. "Can you help me or not?"

"Who is it that you want to talk to?" the door said.

"Iscia," William said.

"Iscia who?" the door asked.

"You know who." William was getting annoyed now.

"Okay," the door said. "I'll see what I can do."

William sat on the bed. He felt numb all over. Passivization really took its toll. He leaned back and lay down, staring at the ceiling like he had done so many times before. He watched the light from the small window as it filtered through the brush outside. It made abstract shapes and forms on the ceiling. The moving shadows relaxed him, and he closed his eyes.

William jolted awake and sat up in bed, looking around the room. He scratched his head. How long had he been asleep?

He looked over at the door. What was it that had woken him?

He swung his legs over the side of the bed and got up. His body was still sore, but he decided to ignore it. A sound from the door made him look—the handle was moving. . . . Someone was trying to get in.

William froze.

"Door . . . ?" he whispered. "Are you there?"

"Shh," the door said. "There's someone out there. You have no scheduled visitors. Stand back."

William stepped away from the door. It was supposed to be burglarproof, so there wasn't any danger, right?

Then the door handle moved again.

"Can't you do something about this?" William asked.

But the door didn't answer.

William looked around for anything he could use to defend himself. His eyes stopped on the chair in front of his desk. His heart sank when he remembered that it was bolted to the floor. His eyes continued to search the room but found nothing.

He could hear someone fiddling with something outside.

"They're opening the door using the code-input panel," the door said.

"Can't you stop them?" William asked.

"They have forehead clearance and the code. There's not much I can do."

"So call a security-bot," William said.

"I did. It'll be here in a couple minutes," the door said. "We're on our own until then. Any ideas?"

"S-s-seriously?" William stammered.

Adrenaline shot through his body as he heard three quick beeps from the door. Then it opened with a click. William had no choice but to stand there and wait.

Nothing happened.

The hall outside was empty.

Suddenly a figure jumped into the doorway. William leaped backward, crashed into the chair behind him, and fell to the floor.

"Hahahahahahaha!" Someone was laughing at him.

William recognized that laugh and looked up.

Iscia was standing by the doorway, giggling so hard she could hardly stay upright. He stared at her. She looked different, more grown-up somehow, even though she was laughing hard.

"That wasn't funny, Iscia," he said, irritated, and got to his feet.

Back home in Norway he had often thought about what he would say to her when he finally saw her again. And what he'd just said was far from what he'd imagined. His face felt hot. He was blushing.

"You should have seen yourself. Your eyes were *soooo* big." She demonstrated with her fingers and chuckled.

They looked at each other for a while. In the end, William couldn't help it. A huge grin spread across his face. He was really pleased to see her again.

"When did you get back?" she asked once her laughter had finally subsided. "And why didn't you let me know?"

"I tried," William said. "They told me you were busy."

"Busy," Iscia said. "I'm not that busy."

"How did you find out I was here?" William said.

"Your door contacted me through the intranet," she said, shutting the door behind her.

"Good," William said, and looked at the door. He knew he could count on it. He rubbed his arm.

"Always nice to have guests anyway," the door said. The hatch opened, and the mechanical arm shot out and held a steaming-hot cupcake in front of Iscia's face.

"Thank you," Iscia said with a surprised smile.

The mechanical hand pulled back, and the hatch in the door snapped shut.

"You seem shaken," Iscia said, taking a bite of the cake. "Did I frighten you that much?"

"I was passivized," William said, scratching his arm.

"It usually itches for hours afterward," she said through a mouthful of cake. "By the way, this is really good." Iscia looked at what was left of the cupcake in her hand.

"Thank you," the door said.

"It doesn't itch, but it's kind of tingly . . . ," William said, still rubbing his arm. "Have you had it done to you?"

"Yeah . . . that was part of our training when we went from being candidates to field assistants," she said. "Being passivized definitely sucks."

William nodded in agreement.

"Why did they secure your room like this?" She looked around, puzzled.

"How did you manage to get in here?" William countered. He didn't want to tell her about his attacks. Not yet.

"It goes with my job. I'm out in the field now. The clearance comes with that."

"So what are you doing now?" William asked. He was dying of curiosity to find out what she was up to.

"It's confidential," she said. "I can't say anything about it."

"I won't tell anyone," William said, disappointed. Was she going to start keeping secrets now too?

"Everything's different now. I'm a field assistant, and I have to follow the rules."

William gave her a hard stare.

"Okay, okay," she said, and smiled. It was like she wanted him to drag it out of her. "I look after stuff . . . ," she said, and paused.

"What stuff?"

"Old stuff."

"Sounds boring." William sat on the bed.

"It's not." She came over and sat next to him, swiveling to face him. "It's old stuff. Some of it's not even supposed to exist. There. Now I've told you. Your turn. Why have they done this to your room?" She looked at the barred window, then down at the bolts that secured the bed to the floor.

William hesitated.

"I have these attacks," he said, and looked away.

"Attacks?" she asked, leaning closer to him. "What kind of attacks?"

"Because of the luridium," William said. "That's why they 'renovated' my room."

"What do you mean?" she asked.

"The luridium is, uh, out of control," William said, avoiding eye contact.

"What do you mean?" she asked again.

"I don't know," William said, squirming. "I get these shooting headaches. Like my head is about to explode . . . and I see things." He stopped, looking at her to check her reaction. He didn't want her to think he was going crazy.

"You see things?" Iscia said. "What kind of things?"

"I don't know," William said. "Strange things. Surreal stuff, like in nightmares. Have you ever had those dreams where you realize that you're dreaming?"

"Yes," Iscia said.

"It's like that," William said. "It feels completely real, but I'm not sure that it is. It's very creepy."

"Do you know what's causing it?" Iscia asked.

"Benjamin is working on something. . . . He made some kind of machine," William said.

"A machine?"

"He called it an audio-sonic regulator."

"A . . . what?" Iscia said.

"It's supposed to duplicate whatever triggers my attacks. It's got something to do with sound waves," William said, and paused for a moment. "At least that's what Benjamin says."

"Don't you trust him?" she asked, peering at him.

"It's more like they don't trust me," William said. "Both him and Goffman."

"Why?" she said.

"Goffman says I'm hallucinating . . . because of the luridium."

"Okay . . . and?"

"I know what I saw," William said. "But Goffman insists that I was hallucinating."

"What are you talking about?" she said, fidgeting.

"I saw something . . . down in the basement."

"Okay. What did you see?" Iscia asked.

"You're going to think I'm crazy too," he said.

"Right, except that I already know you're crazy." She laughed and punched him in the shoulder.

"I saw a man." William stood up. "He was stuck in this metal slab."

Iscia looked at him.

"What are you talking about?" she asked, frowning.

"It was as if the floor had melted and he had sunk into it, like quicksand, before the floor had hardened again." William said.

Iscia sat for a while, gazing into thin air. Her brown eyes grew serious.

"What?" William said. "You don't believe me?"

"I believe you," she said.

"And?" William demanded.

"There was an . . . incident . . . a couple of days ago. At the Institute."

"What incident?" William said.

"It's unclear." Iscia got up. "But there's someone here at the Institute who shouldn't be here . . . an intruder."

"Someone hiding at the Institute?" William said. "Who?"

"They don't know. They picked up a blurry figure on the surveillance cameras. It comes and goes through walls . . . ," she whispered, and gulped. "I don't know any more about it. But it's freaking everyone out."

William stood there, lost in thought. An intruder, here at the Institute? "Come on. I have to show you something," he said, and turned to the door. "Door, we need to get out."

"Not again . . . ," the door said.

"Yes again," William demanded.

"They won't send a porter-bot this late."

"Good," William said, and looked at Iscia. "We won't be needing one."

# 13

**William and Iscia stood in the elevator. It hummed as they** moved down, and gentle Muzak played from a small speaker in the ceiling.

"Level Two B," the elevator announced.

"I'm sure we're going to get in *big* trouble for this," Iscia said as the doors opened with a ding.

"And *I'm* sure this is something you'll want to see," William replied, walking out. "Besides . . . when did getting in a little bit of trouble worry you so much?"

"When they gave me more responsibility," Iscia said, following him.

William sped up. He wanted to get into the laboratory where the old man was before they were discovered.

"It's creepy that someone's sneaking around at the

Institute and no one knows who it is," Iscia said. She shuddered as they moved down the dark hallway.

"I met her," William said.

The words kind of jumped out of his mouth. He had planned on waiting a bit before telling Iscia about the woman who had attacked him. But now it was out there.

"Her?" Iscia said, stopping in her tracks. "Who did you meet?"

"The one they're afraid of," William said. "At least I think it was her."

"A woman?" Iscia asked, and grabbed his arm. "Where did you meet her? At the Institute?"

"No. She attacked me outside my school in Norway," William said. "She wanted me to go with her."

"Wait! Someone tried to kidnap you in Norway?" Iscia said.

"Yes. And Goffman is trying to convince me that it was nothing . . . that we're safe here. But I don't believe him."

"What did she look like?" Iscia asked, her voice getting louder.

"I'll tell you more later when we're not in such a hurry." William continued down the hallway. He liked it when she raised her voice. It meant that she was engaging.

William turned the corner at the end of the hallway. "Okay. Here we are. Use your clearance to open the door."

Iscia stopped next to him.

"I know I'm going to regret this," she whispered.

William looked at her. He could see the glint in her eyes, indicating that part of her was enjoying this adventure.

Iscia walked over to the control panel, leaned in, and put her forehead to the scanner.

A laser beam appeared and traveled a couple of times over her forehead, then disappeared.

"Disapproved," the computer voice said.

Iscia pulled away from the wall, startled.

"That's strange," she said. "I have universal clearance."

She leaned in and repeated the whole procedure but with the same result.

"What's going on?" Iscia asked, baffled.

"They must have changed the codes," William said. "Let me try."

She moved to the side. William focused his attention on the panel. He could feel the vibrations starting at the bottom of his spine.

He closed his eyes and let the vibrations travel up and out into his arms and fingers. He had never gotten completely used to this feeling. It was like there was something controlling his body. And since he'd started having the attacks, the sensation of the luridium moving inside him felt more alien than ever.

William opened his eyes and looked at the control panel. The digits had lit up now. William focused on the glowing numbers, waiting.

At last he saw it. The digits started swapping places. The nine traveled upward on the panel and replaced the three. And so it continued. Like one of those mechanical puzzle games where you move little squares around to make an image. The digits started mixing together, multiplying. Forming long rows of flowing numbers in front of him.

William started pressing the buttons on the control panel. One after another. Faster and faster. And he soon realized that whoever had been fiddling with the control panel since the last time he was here hadn't changed the code. They had deleted it. There was no code anymore. But there was a way around it. A universal code that would probably unlock all the doors at the Institute. And it was this code he had to find now.

His fingers flew across the panel, chasing after the moving digits. The luridium inside him could never completely solve the codes for him. It only gave him clues, and he had to calculate his own way to the answer.

William pressed the final button, and the light disappeared from the digits. The vibrations subsided, and he was back to reality.

He looked at Iscia. Then at the control panel.

Had he cracked the code?

"Approved," a flat voice said from inside the little speaker on the control panel. William shot Iscia a quick look and smiled. She didn't look pleased.

"Oh, you're such a genius," she said.

"It's not your fault." William pushed on the door. "They clearly don't want anyone to go in here."

"So maybe we shouldn't," she said as she peeked into the lab. She was still curious to see what was inside.

"Come on," William said. "But keep an eye out for guard-bots!"

They continued into the room, and the door closed behind them with a metallic click.

*"Whoa,"* Iscia said. "It looks like a space station in here." She stopped short, her eyes scanning the gigantic room. She was clearly impressed.

"What's that over there?" Iscia asked, pointing to the large cannon and the two moveable walls in the middle of the room.

"That's where he is," William answered.

"I don't know if this is such a good idea." She seemed to be having second thoughts.

"I want to hear you say that you can see him too. . . . I have to know that I'm not hallucinating." He pulled her along. He needed to know that he could trust his own senses.

They stopped in front of the curtains.

"Are you ready?" he whispered.

She nodded.

"I should warn you. It's a disturbing sight." William pulled one of the walls aside and gasped.

Iscia burst out laughing.

"It's impossible to get any privacy around here," a flat voice said.

William stood there and stared. The slab and the old man were gone. Instead there was a robot sitting in a deck chair, reading a newspaper.

William remembered the argu-bot from the first time he came to the Institute. It was one of the first robots he had met when he got there. It was designed to be difficult and create arguments.

"What are you doing here?" William asked.

"I could ask the same of you," the argu-bot said. "And not that it's any of your business, but I'm trying to enjoy some hard-earned downtime."

"Where did the old man go?" William demanded, moving closer.

"What old man?" the argu-bot asked, leaning back in his chair.

"The old man who was here," William said. His voice was trembling. "He was stuck in a huge piece of metal."

William turned to Iscia. "This is *not* what I saw," he said. "There *was* an old man."

"I'm not old, and I'm far from retirement," the argu-bot said testily.

William ignored the robot. "They must have moved him." He scanned the floor.

"We should go," Iscia said.

William's eyes landed on a little piece of white plastic on the floor. It lay right under the deck chair where the robot was sitting. It looked like a name tag.

William moved toward the chair.

"What are you doing?" the argu-bot said.

"I need to have a look at something under your chair," William said.

"You need to stop invading my personal space," the argu-bot replied. "I'm very private."

"A quick look," William said.

"That's exactly what my ex-wife used to say," the argu-bot said. "And look where that got me. She ran off with the gardener-bot."

William had had enough—he *had* to get his hands on that name tag.

"Okay, then," William said, and started to turn.

But he pretended to stumble and fell toward the deck chair.

He landed on top of the startled argu-bot and rolled to the floor.

"What are you doing?" the argu-bot yelled. "What about my personal space?"

"I'm sorry," William said as he got to his feet. With a quick movement he pocketed the name tag. He turned to Iscia. "Let's get out of here."

**"William, wait!" Iscia cried, jogging after William as he** strode away down the hallway. "A name tag doesn't prove anything."

"You don't believe me," William said, continuing up the stairs. He looked down at the bit of plastic. It said PONTUS DIPPEL, DEPOSITORY FOR IMPOSSIBLE ARCHAEOLOGY.

"But . . . ," Iscia began, taking the stairs two at a time to catch up with him.

"Do you know who Pontus Dippel is?" William asked.

Iscia hesitated enough for William to realize that she was holding something back. He stopped.

"Do you?" he demanded.

She shook her head and looked down. That only made

William angrier. He turned and continued up the stairs.

"They were holding him captive. I know it," he said. "They experimented on him or tortured him for information. And then they must have moved him somewhere else after I discovered him."

"That's not how the Institute works," Iscia said.

They reached the top of the stairs. William kept striding across the lobby.

"What, like you know everything there is to know about the Institute or something?" William asked.

"I know quite a bit, actually," she said.

"But not everything," William said, stopping again. He turned to face her and waved the name tag in front of her.

"This is enough proof for me that he was there. They're holding him captive somewhere here at the Institute, and I'm going to find out why."

"Find out what?" a voice said from behind him.

William turned around and saw Freddy standing a little way away with a porter-bot. William stuffed the name tag into his pocket. One part of him was surprised to see Freddy still at the Institute; the other was just plain disappointed. Freddy had given him a hard time when William first arrived. And since William had crushed Freddy's orb in a duel, William was sure the other boy wouldn't go any easier on him this time around.

"You're not allowed to move around this place without a porter-bot," Freddy said. "Especially not you." He eyed William through narrow eyes.

"He's with me," Iscia said.

William stared at Freddy's freckled face. He wasn't planning to let him push him around. Freddy had grown since the last time he'd seen him. Now he towered over William, almost a full head taller.

"Leave him alone, Freddy," Iscia said.

Freddy nodded toward the stairs.

"What were you guys doing down there?" he asked.

"We took a wrong turn," William said.

"I would say so," Freddy said with a glance at Iscia.

"Come on," Iscia said, pulling William along.

But Freddy moved in front of them, blocking their way.

"I haven't seen you in a while, William. Where have you been?" Freddy asked, scrutinizing William again with his beady eyes. "I haven't forgotten what you did to my orb."

"Leave him alone, Freddy," Iscia said.

"I just want to say," Freddy whispered, and leaned closer, "that I've forgiven you."

William was caught completely off guard. This was the last thing he'd expected to hear from the Institute's biggest bully.

"You're kidding, right?" The question just slipped out.

"I'm not kidding," Freddy said, and gave William a

fatherly pat on the shoulder. "Orb duels are for children. We're beyond that now. And some of us have become field assistants, too." Freddy glanced over at Iscia with a knowing smile.

William didn't get what was going on. Was Freddy a field assistant now?

"Come on. Let's go," Iscia said, and pulled William along by his arm.

She seemed to be in a real hurry.

"Wait," Freddy said, glancing at Iscia. "You haven't told him . . . have you?"

"I . . . I . . ." Iscia's eyes widened.

William looked at her. Told him what?

"Are you going to say it . . . or should I?" Freddy said.

But Iscia just stood there without saying anything. William looked back at Freddy.

"Iscia and I," Freddy began, and then paused, "are a team now."

A cold shiver ran through William's body. A team?

He gave Iscia a bewildered look.

"We work together," Iscia quickly added. "The Institute teamed us up." She paused for a bit. "I'd been planning to tell you. But you were so preoccupied with . . . with the . . . well, you know . . . that I didn't have a chance to say anything . . ." She was interrupted by a flat computer voice next to them.

"No unapproved loitering in the hallways!"

A guard-bot came rolling toward them, pointing its passivator at them.

"Whoops, I've got to get going," Freddy said with a big grin. "Great to see you again, William." He turned to Iscia. "Are you coming? We're both going the same way, you know." Freddy turned to his porter-bot. "She's coming with us."

The porter-bot nodded.

Iscia turned to William.

"William . . . I . . ." She didn't have a chance to say any more before the guard-bot interrupted her.

"I repeat: You cannot loiter here. Move along."

Freddy and Iscia headed down the hallway with the porter-bot. William stood still, watching them go.

Iscia glanced back at him before they vanished around a corner.

William stared at the empty hallway. What had just happened? He couldn't believe that Iscia had walked away with Freddy.

"You, come with me," the guard-bot said. "I have to take you back to your room."

# 15

**William stopped in front of the large doors that led into the** dining hall.

"There's nothing to see in there," the porter-bot behind him said.

William ignored it. He grabbed the door handle, pulled it toward him, and looked inside.

There was no one there. All the chairs were upside down on the tables. It was a sorry sight. The room should have been bustling with activity right now.

"Like I said," the porter-bot said. "Everyone takes their meals in their rooms now. Because of the security."

William just stood there.

"Benjamin Slapperton is looking for you," the porter-bot said.

William turned to the robot, who held its hand to its ear. A little red lamp on the side of its head flashed. William guessed that a transmission was taking place.

"Does he know where we are?" William asked.

"He's already on his way here," the porter-bot said.

William shut the door and sat on the floor. He leaned against the wall and closed his eyes.

He hadn't slept a wink all night. There were too many things bothering him. The woman with the mechanical hand, the man in the metal slab, and Iscia working with Freddy.

After seeing the old man in the slab with the large cannon over him, William was skeptical about the experiment Benjamin was performing. Did he know what he was doing? Could William trust him? He didn't know if he wanted more tests, and he hated eating breakfast alone in his room. That was why he had come to the cafeteria, but it seemed like he wasn't the only one who had to take his meals in his room. The Institute really had changed, and not for the better.

William looked up as the sound of Benjamin's hovercart came closer. It moved toward him at great speed, slammed into the wall, and stopped.

"I don't want to be out here in the hallways any longer than necessary," Benjamin shouted over the noise from the fan. "And you need to hurry. Something terrible has happened."

"What?" William asked.

"I'll show you when we get back to the lab," Benjamin said, and tapped the empty seat next to him. "Get in!"

After another hair-raising trip through the hallways they were back in the sonic lab.

"It seems to have vanished into thin air during the night," Benjamin said, scratching his head.

William looked at the empty glass cage where the cockroach had been the day before.

"There's no sign of a break-in and nothing on the security cameras. This is an absolute catastrophe. Now we have an out-of-control cockroach filled with luridium running loose around the Institute."

Benjamin shot William a nervous look. "There's no time to lose. We have to hurry."

William nodded.

A few moments later William sat in the chair while Benjamin fiddled with some wires.

"There was an old man in the basement," William said, and turned to Benjamin. "He was stuck in a metal slab. And there was a cannon like that one pointing at him." William nodded at the cannon in the ceiling.

Benjamin, who was on all fours fiddling with some wires inside the control box, stopped what he was doing. "I don't know anything about that." It sounded rehearsed.

"And then, when I went back there, the old man was gone," William said.

"You shouldn't roam around the Institute like that on your own," Benjamin said, and closed the lid on the side of the box. "What if you had an attack?" He got to his feet and gave William a serious look. "It's dangerous. We should begin."

William felt Benjamin's hand on his shoulder.

"I know that all this is difficult."

William looked up at him.

"I'm not doing this to hurt you. I'm trying to help," Benjamin said. "If I thought there was any chance of danger to you, I wouldn't put you through this." Benjamin smiled. "We have to find out what's causing your attacks."

Benjamin pointed at the straps on each armrest. "Since the last time, I've added some more of these and one for your waist. It's for your own safety. Do you mind?"

William gulped.

"Okay . . . ," he said.

Benjamin strapped William's hands to the armrests. Then he fastened a belt around William's waist. He gave William a quick pat on the shoulder and returned to the control box.

"Are you ready?" he asked.

William nodded.

"After what happened the last time, I've made this for you." Benjamin passed William a little black box with a red button on it. "For the sake of the experiment, I need you to bear it for as long as you can. But if it becomes to much for you, press the button, and the cannon will turn off. Okay?"

William nodded again. He tensed his fingers around the little box, leaned back in the chair, and closed his eyes. He felt Benjamin put the headphones on him, and then everything became quiet.

A few minutes later the machine above him started humming.

At first the noise was so faint that he could hardly hear it. Then the volume increased in strength, becoming louder. Soon William could feel the sound waves traveling through his body, and then the rumbling at the base of his spine began.

Then came the cold.

It spread up his back and out into his arms. William tightened his grip on the little box with the red button. He didn't want to press it . . . not yet. He wanted to see what would happen next.

The cold continued out into his hands, and then the headache struck. It was as if someone had shot him in the forehead with an arrow. He gritted his teeth together, trying not to scream. He had to fight to keep from pressing the red button. His hands shook, and he had problems holding on to the remote control.

*Must not press . . . must not press . . .*

The rumbling disappeared, and everything went quiet.

When William opened his eyes again, he was standing in the big cavernous hall with high stone walls.

As before, a large golden ring hovered above the space.

William spotted something standing on the ground below the golden ring. It was the same white coffin that he'd seen before. There was something menacing about the oblong box. And William still felt like he should know what the box was. . . .

He pulled back as the lid on the box opened. A frosty mist seeped out and weaved its way down toward the floor like a snake. A hand appeared from inside the box. William wanted to turn away. Close his eyes. But he couldn't. He stood there, staring at the hand.

"WILLIAM?" someone shouted from the darkness.

William opened his eyes.

He was back in the lab at the Institute.

"WILLIAM?" he heard someone shout again. His headphones made it hard to hear where the sound was coming from.

Suddenly he saw Benjamin floating in the air in front of him, a few yards above the floor. Slapperton flailed his arms like crazy and pointed at William.

"PUSH THE BUTTON!"

William looked down at the little remote control he was still holding in his hand. He punched down the button with his thumb, and the sound cannon stopped humming. The cold in his body disappeared, and Benjamin crashed to the floor.

"I know what's causing it," Benjamin said, getting to his feet. "I know what's causing it."

"What is it?" William asked, and tried to get out of the chair. But the straps held him back.

Benjamin hurried over to his desk. With shaky hands, he searched through the clutter before he found a small notepad and a pencil. He wrote something on the pad, tore the page off, and stuffed it into his pocket.

"What did you find out?" William shouted, as Benjamin still had his protective ear gear on.

"Sorry," Benjamin said, and hurried back to William. He removed the straps around William's wrists and waist and helped him out of the chair. "I have to do some more calculations," he said. "But I'll tell you as soon as I've figured it out."

"But you said that you knew what it was," William said, rubbing his wrist.

"Yes," Benjamin said. "I found a sub-frequency of sound waves that causes levitation." He took a short pause. "And there's only one source that I know of that has been known to produce waves like that. But if it is what I think it is . . . it's impossible."

"Impossible?" William said.

"Yes," Benjamin said. "Impossible."

# 16

**William sat on his bed, staring into space.**

He had barely slept the night before, and he now had a pounding headache.

He thought about what he had seen during the attack. The mysterious floating ring and the figure in the box. What did it mean? Somehow he knew that it had to do with Abraham and his cryogenic box. But what was that huge golden ring? And what was it Benjamin had discovered? He said he had found out what was behind William's attacks . . . but that it was impossible. What on earth was he talking about?

William got up and walked over to the window. Tracked vehicles were still patrolling the white wall that fenced in the vast park, and a surveillance drone whizzed past his window.

As he stood there, lost in his own thoughts, he sensed something in the room. A faint tapping somewhere behind him. William turned around and listened. The tapping was gone. Then it began again. This time louder.

William took a step forward but froze as a cockroach shot across the floor in front of him. The insect scurried toward a dark corner at the other side of the room. And that's when William saw it. Someone was standing in the corner, completely still. The cockroach stopped, and the figure bent down, positioning its mechanical hand so the cockroach could climb onto it. Then the person straightened up again and looked at William.

It felt like time had stopped. The familiar smell of burned rubber overwhelmed him, and he felt like he couldn't breathe . . . like the air in the room had become toxic.

William groped around for something to defend himself with, but his hand found only air. He backed up and hit the wall by the window. He stood there completely paralyzed, staring at the figure, which took a step toward him.

William gasped.

It was the same woman who had attacked him outside his school.

She was wearing dark sunglasses, and her wild, dirty hair covered half her face. Her mechanical hand was covered in strange symbols William had never seen before.

"It hurts," the woman said in a raspy voice.

"What hurts?" The words fell out of William's mouth.

"Not belonging," the woman said. "Being in the middle."

"The middle?" William said.

She removed her dark sunglasses. Her eyes were intense and looked completely crazy. One of them darted back and forth as if it were following an invisible fly. William caught a glimpse of the other side of her face. The skin was curled and red as if it had been badly burned at some point in the past.

"You're a freak, William, like me. You're neither human nor machine. You're just . . . in the middle. You're basically . . . nothing."

William had to concentrate to keep from panicking completely, but the adrenaline surging through his body made it impossible to think clearly.

"I thought I had lost it for good," she said, and held up the cockroach. "Then I stumbled across it here, in one of the laboratories. Isn't that crazy?"

William just stood there. He didn't know what to say . . . or do.

"This little thing has enough luridium in it to tip the scale. All it takes is for you to touch it, and the luridium would leave its little body and enter yours. Then you would be more machine than human. That would have been much better for you. Then you would at least be . . . something."

William looked at the insect. And for a split second he

considered how it would be to join the other side. It was like this woman had some kind of hypnotic effect on him. When she talked, it was as if her voice came from inside *his* head, almost as though she could speak directly to his brain.

"A shame you'll never get to it. I would never let you hurt it. We've been friends for a long time."

"How did you get in here?" William asked, casting a quick glance at the door. It was closed.

"I have my ways," she said, and grinned.

"What do you want?" William said, trying to hide the tremble in his voice.

"Like I said outside your stupid school," the woman said, baring her teeth, "I need you to do something for me."

"Do what?"

"They haven't told you about what happened in the Depository?" she asked. "Keeping it all a *biiiig* secret." She gestured with her arms.

"What happened in the basement?" William asked. But he was pretty sure that he knew what she was talking about.

"You've already seen it," she said.

"The man in the slab?" William asked.

She didn't respond, just stood there watching him with a smirk on her lips.

William studied her, searching for some sign that she was a product of his own brain playing a trick on him. Another hallucination.

"If you help me," she said, "I can make your attacks go away."

William's heart pumped so hard now, it felt like it would jump right out of his chest.

He had to buy some more time.

"What is it you want me to do?" he asked.

"It's still here . . . at the Institute," she whispered, and shot a quick look around the room, like she was talking about a big secret.

"What?" William said.

"You'll know when you see it," she said. "I've made some arrangements."

"KNOCK, KNOCK," the door said.

The woman turned to the door and hissed. Then she raised her mechanical hand.

"I'll see you again soon, William Wenton," she whispered, and pushed one of the buttons. The hand began emitting a high-pitched sound. "If you tell anyone about me . . . I won't be so nice next time we meet. I might even take it out on your little girlfriend."

"Leave Iscia alone!" William shouted.

And with a zap and a flash of blue light the woman was gone.

Only smoke and a sickening smell of burned rubber lingered in the air. William knew that she would be back. But for now he was safe and had some time to think.

"KNOCK . . . KNOCK," the door repeated before opening.

Iscia stood outside. A porter-bot lingered in the background.

"I feel so bad," she said, smiling apologetically.

William swallowed and tried to compose himself.

"Why?" he said.

"Because of what happened yesterday . . . about Freddy . . . and me not telling you . . ."

"That's okay," William said, his voice shaking.

"Are you all right?" Iscia asked, and looked at him. "Is something burning?" She sniffed the air.

"Everything's great," William said, and pushed past her into the hallway, closing the door behind him.

"You sure?" she said. "You seem . . . upset."

William shook his head, unsure what to say.

"There's something I want to show you," Iscia said.

"What?" William said.

"Something about Pontus Dippel," she replied.

"The old man?"

She gave him a quick nod and started walking.

# 17

Soon William and Iscia were jogging through the park behind the Institute.

Iscia dodged behind bushes and around trees with rehearsed movements. William followed close behind her.

The sun was setting, causing the tall trees to cast long, dark shadows across the grass. They had managed to sneak away from their porter-bot. It was probably buzzing around in confusion somewhere at the Institute, looking for them. But now they had a different problem: all the security vehicles out in the park.

William was still shaken from meeting the woman in his room. What was it she wanted him to do?

He would have to find a way to protect himself, but he didn't want to tell Iscia about what had happened. He didn't want to put her in danger until he knew what they were up against.

"Things ended on kind of a rough note last time," Iscia said. "I don't want you to think I'm hiding things from you, so I want to show you what we've been up to."

"We . . . as in you and Freddy?" William asked.

"We didn't have any choice. The Institute assigned us to work together," Iscia said. "Freddy's not so bad once you get to know him. It was his idea to take you here."

"Really?" William asked.

"Yes," she said as she stopped and took him by the arm.

She pulled him down behind a large shrub, then put her finger to her lips. They stayed still and waited. All William could hear was his own breathing. Then a small tank with a passivator on its roof stopped right in front of the bush they were hiding behind. William could see it through the green brush. A camera mounted next to the little cannon swept over the area. It didn't appear to have seen them, because it drove off again.

"They have motion detectors," Iscia whispered. "If we hold completely still, they have a hard time detecting us."

"Where are we going?" William said.

"There," she said, pointing to the man-made pond in the middle of the park. "Come on." Iscia checked to see if the coast was clear before she got to her feet and continued.

William got up and darted after her. It felt good to be

out in the fresh air after spending so much time alone in his room. It also felt good being with Iscia again.

Soon they were running along the water's edge.

The surface of the water was covered with white lilies. A little way out in the pond there was a statue of a woman holding a lamp in the shape of an orb over her head. The orb gave off a golden light.

A couple of swans paddled past the statue. William stopped and stood there, watching them. They stood out in sharp contrast to the rest of the park, which now resembled the exercise yard in a prison. He was struck by how beautiful and majestic they looked.

"Come on," Iscia whispered. "They get suspicious pretty quickly."

"Who?" William asked, glancing around.

"The swans," Iscia said, pointing. "You don't want to get on their bad side."

One of the swans had turned around and was staring right at William with glowing red eyes.

"What, are you afraid of swans now?" William teased her with a grin.

"Those aren't normal swans," Iscia said.

William looked at the white birds again. One of the swans approached them, fluffing its feathers. A little cannon popped up from a hatch on its back.

"They're cyborg swans!" William said, startled.

"Of course," Iscia said, tugging at him. "If we stand here for very long, they'll shoot. We have to get in there before they realize that you're not Freddy." She pointed to a stone gazebo by the edge of the water a little farther away. Two guard-bots with passivators stood in front of the entrance.

"There are guard-bots there," William said.

"I know," Iscia said. "They've been there since it happened."

"What happened?" William asked.

But Iscia was scurrying toward the gazebo.

William cast a glance back over his shoulder. Both swans were staring at them now and had their cannons pointed in their direction. One of the big birds had already reached the shore and was stepping out of the water.

William and Iscia raced alongside the shore until they reached the gazebo. Iscia stopped in front of a solid-looking brass door. It had to be old, because it was covered with scratches and oxidation. There was a dial in the middle of the door, like on a safe.

"Halt," one of the guard-bots called out, and raised the passivator it was clutching in its metal hands.

"We have clearance," Iscia said.

The other guard-bot scanned her forehead. The lamp on the scanner changed color from red to green.

"What about him?" the guard-bot said, and pointed at William.

"He's with me," Iscia said.

"You may pass," the guard-bot said, and rolled to the side.

William stepped closer and ran his fingers over the rough surface of the door. He felt the rumbling begin in his stomach, the way it did whenever he faced a code.

"That's old," he said, fascinated.

"Yes," Iscia said. "Very old. It took me more than two weeks to crack it. It was one of the entrance requirements."

Iscia looked over at the two swans that were waddling toward them.

"We'd better hurry. The swans are smarter than the guard-bots," she whispered, and turned the dial, first one way and then the other until there was a faint click.

The door slid open on its rusty hinges.

William cast one last glance back at the swans before following Iscia inside and pulling the door shut behind him.

They were standing in pitch-darkness inside the little gazebo now.

Iscia placed her forehead to a control panel on the wall next to a pair of elevator doors.

The doors slid open with a soft ding.

"Come on," Iscia said, and motioned for him to follow her into the elevator.

# 18

**William and Iscia were standing in a large glassed-in room** with a vaulted ceiling.

It looked like an upside-down aquarium. William realized that they had to be underneath the pond where the swans had been swimming. Faint sunlight glimmered through the murky water above them. Something that looked like a mechanical shark swam past the window.

"This room belongs to the old part of the Institute that was built more than a hundred years ago," Iscia said. "The dome's made of shatter-resistant glass. This is where the Institute keeps some of the most secret objects."

"Is this the Depository?" William asked. He stared into the darkness. He could make out the contours of various objects ahead of them. He looked down at the floor and stomped his foot. The whole floor seemed to be made of steel. Here and there, patches of rust had formed from occasional leaks from the glass dome above.

"Yes," Iscia said. "To be more precise: the Depository for Ancient Items No One Can Explain. That's my unofficial name anyway."

She pressed a switch on the wall, and an old brass light fixture in the ceiling flickered to life. William gasped as the room lit up, revealing the many objects that lay in front of them.

At first glance the items looked like normal old things you would find in any history museum. But as William began strolling around, he could see they were so much more.

"Don't touch anything," Iscia warned.

His eyes rested on something sitting alone in a small case, and he stopped short.

"Is that what I think it is?" he asked, so excited his voice was shaking.

"That depends on what you think it is," Iscia said with a smile.

"The London hammer . . . ," he whispered, looking at the item in the case.

"Correct."

Inside the case was a rusty old hammer with a wooden handle. It didn't look special—just a hammer that had been left in the rain for decades—but William had read about it in one of his grandfather's books back home in Norway.

Called the London hammer, it had been found by an elderly married couple out for a walk in a place called London, Texas. They had spotted a wooden handle sticking out of a rock. They thought that was odd and took it home with them before sending it to a lab. The scientists opened the rock and found an entire hammer inside.

"Do you think it's true . . . what they discovered?" William asked without taking his eyes off the hammer.

"That it's so old?" Iscia said.

"Yeah."

"Millions of years old?" she said. "The hammer had been trapped inside the dirt for so long that the dirt itself had hardened and become rock. That's a process that takes millions of years."

"That's long before there were people," William said. "Which in principle should be impossible."

"That's why it's here," Iscia said. "Everything in here is somehow impossible in one way or another. At least based on what we know about the history of humans on earth."

William had to force himself away from the hammer and to continue among the display cases. When he reached a massive oblong glass case in the middle of the room, he gasped.

"That can't be real!" he said.

"It is," she said.

There was a gigantic human skeleton lying in the case in front of them. William walked over to the skull and studied it through the glass. The skull alone was as tall as he was. He looked down the length of the enormous body. The arms were stretched out along its sides. He'd seen pictures online of gigantic skeletons like this, but most of them were later revealed to be fakes.

"How old is it?" he asked.

"The tests that were run indicated an approximate age of around four hundred million years," she said.

William noticed a wide crack in the skull's forehead.

"What's that?" he asked, pointing.

"The cause of death, I assume," she said. "It must have fallen or been hit on the head by something heavy. This skeleton was donated to us from an anonymous private collector in Egypt. He didn't feel safe holding on to it any longer. Impossible archaeology is a very dangerous business."

"Why?" William asked.

Iscia hesitated. "Because there are a lot of people out there who don't want the truth to come out," she finally said.

William looked at her. "What truth?"

"The truth about our whole history as a species on this planet," Iscia said.

"What do you mean?" William asked, looking at her.

"For a start, we have been on earth much longer than most people think." Iscia was almost whispering now.

"And how long is that?" William asked.

"Look around," she said, and pointed at all the ancient objects that surrounded them. "Many of these man-made objects are millions of years old."

"So?" William said. "Does it matter how long we've been here?"

"It matters to a lot of people," Iscia said. "Could you imagine the ramifications if it came out that humans have been on earth millions, instead of hundreds of thousands of years? Our whole history would have to be rewritten."

"I get it," William said. "People aren't ready for the truth."

"Something like that," she said. "So we keep it stored and catalogued here, until one day it becomes . . . public."

"When the public is ready?" William added.

Iscia nodded.

William thought it was strange that part of humanity's history had to be hidden away. That it could even be considered dangerous. Why was it that people found things that were out of the ordinary so threatening? What were they afraid of?

William thought about the luridium in his own body. That made him unusual too. He remembered how his teacher back home in Norway treated him. William knew it was because Mr. Humburger feared him. Was it because he sensed that William was different? He knew that William was smarter than him in some ways. Maybe people weren't ready for him, either.

He looked at the giant skeleton.

"He must have been more than thirty feet tall," he said.

"She," Iscia said. "She was female."

"Wow," William said. "Do you think there were giants on earth?"

"After I started working here, I realized one thing," Iscia said, and paused.

"What was that?"

"That most things are possible. I thought you'd like seeing this." She moved farther into the space. "What do you think about that over there?" she asked, pointing.

William's mouth dropped open when he saw what Iscia was pointing to. Leaning against the far wall was a large glass cabinet. And inside it was something that looked like a stone robot.

He stopped in front of the cabinet and read the sign. He recognized his grandfather's swooping handwriting: *3.8-million-year-old exoskeleton.*

"That's one of the oldest exoskeletons we've found," Iscia said.

"Three point eight million years old?" William mumbled in disbelief. "Who made it?"

"We're not sure," Iscia said.

"How was it powered?" William asked. "Electricity?"

"I have no idea," Iscia said, and scratched her head. "And neither does Benjamin or anyone else here at the Institute.

They collect all this stuff from around the world and bring it here for further examination. Then they try to replicate the most interesting technology. They have done lots of work on exoskeletons like this one."

"I know," William said. "They sent one to my father. It's really cool."

William let his eyes wander over the various cabinets in the room. He wasn't sure what he thought about all this. If even one of the items in here was authentic, it would rewrite world history. He was beginning to understand why there were so many people who wanted to keep these discoveries under wraps.

"I'm sorry I didn't believe you," Iscia said.

He turned around and looked at her.

"You mean about the man in the slab?" William said.

She nodded.

"You're not crazy," she said. "He's real."

William waited for her to continue.

"Pontus Dippel was the curator of all this," she said.

William remembered what it had said on the name tag: Depository for Impossible Archeology.

"Come over here," she said, motioning to him. "There's something else I want to show you."

# 19

**"That's where they found him,"** Iscia said, pointing at the floor in front of them.

There was a large square hole in the floor. William estimated that the hole was about the same size as the slab the old man had been stuck in.

"What happened to him?" William said.

"Someone ambushed him and shot him with some kind of ray," Iscia said. "It was meant to kill him, but he survived. However, he was fused into the floor. They had to cut out a block and move him to a laboratory, where they're trying to free him."

"Why didn't you tell me this before?" William asked.

"It's supposed to be top secret," she said. "But I'm telling you now. That must count for something?"

William nodded, walking over to the edge and looking into the hole.

"Do you know who did it?" he asked.

She shook her head.

"Do you know why?" William said.

Iscia was about to answer, when she was interrupted by the sound of footsteps.

William turned and saw Freddy coming toward them. Iscia moved to stand beside William as Freddy came over and stopped, looking at William.

"Exciting . . . isn't it?" Freddy threw out his arms like a king showing someone his kingdom. "All this fantastic tech. And that hole." He pointed at the square hole in the floor. "Someone materialized from nowhere and zapped poor old Pontus into the floor. I knew you'd find this place interesting. With all the codes and stuff."

William didn't say anything. He still didn't understand why Freddy was acting so friendly. It was a big contrast to the last time he had been at the Institute.

Freddy looked at Iscia. "Did you show him the orb yet?" he asked.

"What orb?" She looked puzzled.

"William loves orbs." Freddy walked past the hole and in between two large shelves. "Come on. I'll show him!"

William looked at Iscia.

"We should leave," she said.

William felt a faint tingling in his belly.

It grew in strength, and the vibrations started traveling up his spine.

It wasn't an attack.

It was that other feeling . . . the one he got when he was tackling codes. It was like an invisible force pulled him forward, and he had no choice but to start walking.

"Where are you going?" he heard Iscia say from behind him.

"I don't know. Something's happening."

He moved through the various display cases in the same direction Freddy had gone, stopping when he got to the other end of the room. It was darker there and seemed to be a less used part of the storage.

William stood there as the vibrations filled his body. In front of him were rows of old glass cabinets. Some of them were covered with dusty cotton tarps.

"Where did Freddy go?" Iscia asked, stopping next to William.

"Dunno," William said, trying to control his vibrations.

"This is the really old stuff," Iscia said.

"I thought everything down here was old?"

"This stuff is so old, it's undatable," she said.

"Over here." Freddy's voice came from somewhere in the darkness.

William moved in the direction of Freddy's voice. His

eyes had adapted to the dark now, and he spotted Freddy standing by an old cabinet.

The cabinet was twice William's height, about two yards wide, and covered with a gray tarpaulin.

Freddy raised his hand and grabbed hold of the sheet, pulling it off.

"I don't think you should . . . ," Iscia began.

Whatever it was inside the cabinet, it was having a strong effect on William. It had to be some kind of code.

Now he could make out the contours of the object in the case: It was round, about the size of a basketball. He took a step closer and leaned in until his forehead stopped at the glass. His eyes were locked on the object.

It was an orb.

It looked like it was made from brass and was covered in strange symbols and full of deep dents and cuts.

William could feel the vibrations all over now, and more than anything he wanted to hold the orb in his hands.

"That thing has to be really old," he mumbled.

"It is," Freddy said. "Priceless . . ."

"So let it be," Iscia said. "If we broke it, we would get in big trouble."

William tried to fight the urge to open the cabinet door and lift the orb out. What would be the harm in taking a look at it? He wanted to but stopped himself.

He forced himself to take a couple of steps back. The vibrations subsided a little.

"Where did it come from?" William asked without taking his eyes off the orb.

"I don't know," Iscia said. "It's been here forever. All the stuff in this end of the room has."

"Should we take it out for a closer look?" Freddy said. "I've always wondered what that orb could do."

"No," William said. "We should leave."

"Why?" Freddy said. "Everything has become so serious around here. Won't hurt to have a little fun. You're the genius, William. Now's our chance to find out what that orb is all about."

"It's old and fragile." Iscia moved to throw the tarpaulin over the cabinet again, but Freddy stopped her.

"I'm sure William would love to have a look at it," Freddy said. "Wouldn't you, William?" Freddy looked at William.

"I'd better not," William said.

"You're being modest." Freddy flicked up the latch on the glass door and reached in for the orb. It seemed heavy. He lifted it out and held it in both hands.

"This is the real deal," he said. "Not like the fake ones they give us here at the Institute." He stared at it for a moment.

"They confiscated all the orbs," Freddy said, his eyes

fixed on William. "Did you know that they confiscated them all?"

William shook his head. He didn't. "Why?" he asked.

"Something about security," Freddy said, and looked at the old orb he held in his hands. "Orbs are powerful things. But you already knew that, William."

"You should put it back," Iscia said.

"Why?" Freddy said. "Let him solve it and see what happens." He nodded to William. "No harm in solving something that old."

"Cut it out, Freddy," Iscia said, irritated. She tried to take the orb from him, but Freddy pulled it away.

"What do you say, William?" Freddy goaded him. "Don't you want to try it? It's bound to be too old to work anyway."

"Don't listen to him, William," Iscia said, pulling him by the arm.

But William was transfixed. His whole body still vibrated. It was as if the old orb was drawing him closer. He could already feel the vibrations starting in his stomach again.

Before he knew it, he had taken the orb from Freddy's hands. It felt cold and heavy. The vibrations spread up his spine and into his arms the instant he touched it.

"William?" he heard Iscia say.

But it was too late now. Her voice sounded like it was coming from far away. And William was already going into his code-breaking state.

His fingers set to work. The various parts were difficult to move at first—it had obviously been a long time since the orb had been used—but little by little as he twisted and turned them, the parts began to slide. *Click . . . click . . . click.* Faster and faster.

William glanced at Freddy. He was standing over by Iscia, who was watching William with concern.

What was he doing? After all, they didn't know the first thing about this orb or what it could do.

He looked down at his fingers, which were flying over the orb. He tried to stop them, make them cut it out, but they kept working. They wouldn't obey him. William tried harder. He pulled one hand back with all his might. His hand let go, and the orb fell to the floor.

William stood there, staring at the orb lying motionless in front of him.

"If it's ruined, it's your fault," Freddy said.

"You're the one who egged him on, you fool," Iscia said. "Come on, William. Let's go. Before he makes you do some other dumb things."

Then the orb began to vibrate, like a drumroll.

"What's happening?" Freddy asked, backing away.

"I don't know," William said.

He regretted having let Freddy dare him into trying to solve the orb.

The orb's vibrations increased, growing louder.

"If it keeps going like that, it's going to punch a hole in the floor," Freddy said.

"Look . . . it's levitating," Iscia said, staring at the orb wide-eyed.

And sure enough, the orb rose off the floor and floated upward. When it reached the height of William's head, it stopped and hovered there in midair.

"I don't like this," Freddy said. "Should we call someone?"

"Who are we going to call? Your mom?" Iscia asked, irritated. "This is your fault."

"Let's get out of here," Freddy said, and started to go.

"We can't leave it like this," William said.

"Well, turn it off, then." Freddy looked like he was about to cry.

"I don't think that will work," William said.

The orb, which was still hovering in front of them, was vibrating faster and faster. It was making a high-pitched beeping sound now. The noise reminded William of the sound cannon in Benjamin's lab.

Then William felt it. The cold that grew in the pit of his stomach and then started to spread through his body . . . the stabbing headache . . . One of those awful attacks was starting again.

He turned to Iscia. "Get out of here . . . and get Benjamin."

"Huh?" Iscia didn't understand. "What are you talking about?"

"He said get out of here." Freddy was already moving.

The display cases around them started creaking. William looked down at his feet and realized his body was floating off the floor.

"Help!" Freddy screamed. He was also rising up in the air now.

"It reverses the force of gravity," William shouted back, pointing at the hovering orb. "It's going to destroy everything in here!"

"But everything is bolted down," Iscia cried over the noise.

She was hanging upside down, clinging to the edge of one of the display cases. William was already hovering several feet above the ground. He searched desperately for something to hold on to.

"Get out of here!" he shouted again.

He felt the attack taking over and the cold spreading to his hands. He struggled to remain conscious and had a hard time controlling his movements. It felt like his body was vibrating in time with the orb.

"What's happening to you?" he heard Iscia yell.

But William couldn't answer. Everything around him grew foggy.

He was back in the cave. There was the floating Hula-Hoop

he had seen during his other attacks. The hovering hoop vibrated violently and emitted a bright golden light. The white box stood on the floor under it. There was no one else there.

The vibrations from the ring increased, and the box started to levitate. It started upward toward the hoop.

Then stopped midway.

William knew that this wasn't good.

What had he done?

# 20

**William tried to gain control of his thoughts.**

Slowly things were coming back to him. The old orb . . . the Depository . . . weightlessness.

He forced his eyes open and looked around. He was lying in a bed.

But he wasn't in his room. This room was much bigger and completely white with beds along the walls. The two chauffeurs stood guard by the room's single door.

William started when he saw a figure standing by the window. He tried to sit up but collapsed back on the bed. He was still dizzy, and he had a terrible headache. The figure came toward him.

"What happened down there?" Goffman asked. He didn't sound particularly pleased. "Most of the items in the Depository that weren't bolted to the floor were destroyed."

"Destroyed?" William asked, confused.

"Yes . . . destroyed." Goffman stopped by the end of the bed.

"What about Iscia . . . and Freddy?" William said. "Is Iscia all right?"

"They'll survive," Goffman said. "But there will be consequences for bringing you down there."

Goffman leaned his cane against a chair and strode around the bed, stopping right next to William. He leaned over and stared at him.

"I guess you finally found out about Pontus Dippel," Goffman said.

William nodded. "How was he melted into the floor like that?"

"That's what we're trying to find out," Goffman said. "I don't think he was meant to survive, but somehow he did. Now we're waiting for him to wake up so he can tell us who it was. And why they did it."

"What about the surveillance cameras?" William asked.

"Nothing." Goffman looked up at a surveillance camera on the wall. It pointed directly at William's bed. "Whoever it was must have had some kind of scrambling technology." He sounded frustrated. "Tell me what happened down there!" he finally said.

William looked over at the two chauffeurs. They made him uneasy.

"Do they have to be here?" he asked.

Goffman nodded to the androids, who turned and left the room. Goffman was quiet for a moment before he continued. "I need to know what you did that made everything levitate."

William lay there for a moment.

"It was down there," William said. "In between all the old stuff."

"What was?" Goffman said.

"The orb," William said.

"Orb?" Goffman's eyes opened wide, as if what William had just said frightened him. He sat in a chair by the bed and motioned for William to continue.

"A very old orb," William said, sitting up.

"There's been only one orb down at the Depository," he said. "And that was stolen when Pontus was attacked. What did this orb look like?"

"It was quite big," William said. "About the size of a basketball." He showed with his hands. "Covered in scratches and dents."

Goffman just sat there. The little color he had in his face drained away. He looked like he had been told the earth was about to come to an end.

"I wanted to have a look at it," William said. "Then everything sort of happened. . . ."

"They must have put it back," Goffman mumbled to himself. "And you solved it?" he asked.

William nodded. He felt like an idiot. How could he have been so stupid? How could he have let Freddy trick him into solving the orb?

William looked down at his hands.

It wasn't until now, when it was all quiet, that he heard it. A faint sound. He had heard it before.

*Puff . . . puff . . . puff . . .*

William looked around. At first he had thought that he was the only patient here, but now he saw that the bed curtains were closed around one of the other beds nearby.

"That sound," William said, looking at Goffman. "I've heard it before."

"That's right," Goffman said. "We finally managed to defragment him. He's in an artificial coma now. And we're waiting for him to wake up."

William thought of the woman who had appeared in his room. He had held back from telling anyone about her. He was afraid Goffman would say it was another figment of his illusory mind. But now William had proof that the old man was real. That meant the woman had to be too.

"There's something else . . . ," he started, but stopped when the door was flung open. Benjamin stormed into the room. He flailed his hands and looked around until he spotted William and Goffman.

"You're not going to believe this," he shouted, running toward them.

"What?" Goffman asked, getting up from the chair.

"I had a suspicion," Benjamin said, screeching to a halt by the bed. "But I had no way to prove it. But during that last wave when . . . when William had his last attack, I pinpointed the source. And it confirmed what I thought."

"Confirmed what?" Goffman said.

"It's real," Benjamin said. His voice was trembling with excitement. "It's real. And it's been activated."

"What's activated?" Goffman said.

"The Crypto Portal," Benjamin said.

"The Crypto Portal?" Goffman repeated. "That's impossible."

"That's exactly what I said," Benjamin said.

Goffman stood still for what seemed like forever; only his eyes darted back and forth. William thought that he had suffered a breakdown.

"Of course." Goffman looked at William. "You activated the portal when you solved the orb."

"What portal?" William asked.

Goffman didn't answer. He grabbed Benjamin and started for the door, then stopped as if he'd thought of something. He turned and looked at William. "You stay here. The guard-bots will keep an eye on you. Don't move."

Goffman opened the door, and two guard-bots waiting

outside wheeled into the room. Both had passivators.

And before William knew it, Goffman and Benjamin were gone.

His thoughts were racing inside his head.

What was the Crypto Portal?

# 21

**William looked over at the guard-bots by the door, then at** the bed where Pontus Dippel was lying. Because of the curtains, he couldn't see the old man.

Did Goffman expect William to just lie there and not do anything? Especially now, when everything seemed to be crumbling around him?

His thoughts returned to what he'd experienced during the attack. The large golden ring and the levitating freezer. William tried to make sense of things, but it only made his headache worse. He looked at the rows of windows in front of him. He should try to open one of them. He really needed some fresh air. Then it hit him: the smell of burned rubber. He knew exactly what that meant.

"William," a hoarse voice said from somewhere in the room.

A paralyzing fear spread through him. William looked around and spotted a figure over by the window.

It was her again. She grinned and took a step toward him.

"HALT!" one of the guard-bots commanded, and raised its passivator.

With a quick zap, the woman evaporated both robots with the ray from her mechanical hand. She opened the lid on the arm and poured the metal dust onto the floor.

"They never learn," she said, coming closer.

She was carrying a heavy-looking leather bag.

The woman pushed a button on the mechanical hand, and, with a zap, she disappeared. William looked around. She was gone. His heart beat feverishly as he sat up farther.

With another zap, the woman reappeared right at the foot of his bed. William jumped back and slammed into the wall behind him.

"What do you want?" he asked. His voice trembling.

"I've already gotten what I want." She walked around the bed. Her leather boots squeaked with each step she took. She stopped right next to him and sat down on the edge of the bed. The smell of burned rubber was unbearable.

"What did you get?" William pushed himself back against the headboard. All he wanted was to move away from her.

"This." The woman held up the leather bag and set it on her lap. She grinned.

"What's that?" William asked.

She unzipped the bag and opened it so he could see inside.

"The orb?" he blurted out. It was the same orb Freddy had tricked him into solving down at the Depository. Her little cockroach scurried across it and hid deeper down in the bag.

"First I stole the orb from the Depository," she said. "I needed you to solve it for me. As you know now, it's protected by codes."

"That's why you approached me outside my school?" William asked.

"Of course," she said. "But your grandfather got to you first and brought you back here, so I had to improvise. I put the orb back where I stole it from. I thought it would be the last place they would look for it. I was right. Then I made some arrangements . . . and bingo." She threw out her arms. "I finally got you to do what I wanted. . . ." She looked affectionately down at the orb, stroking it like it was a kitten. "The Institute had it down there all these years and didn't even know what it was. I've been trying to solve it, but not everyone can be a code-breaking genius like you."

"But what does it do?" William said.

"This orb," she said, tapping the bag with her metal hand, "activates the Crypto Portal in the Himalayas. It's like a remote control."

"The Crypto Portal?" William repeated, confused. He remembered Benjamin's reaction before he and Goffman had stormed out. He had talked about the Crypto Portal being activated.

"Those fools at the Institute didn't expect a thing. They thought that the portal was destroyed millions of years ago. But it wasn't." She paused briefly and stared at William with her wild eyes. "And now I'm going to send him through it."

"Him?" William asked.

"I might as well tell you." She grinned. "Before I dispose of you." She pushed a button on her arm. "You've done what I wanted you to do, and I really don't need you anymore. You're worth more to me dead than alive now."

William pushed himself up against the wall. Was she really going to shoot him with that hand of hers?

"I thought that someone with your mental abilities would have figured it out by now," she said, pointing her metal arm at him.

"What?" William asked. His voice trembled now, and adrenaline rushed through his body.

"Because I did what they thought was impossible," she said. "What they thought would never happen . . ."

"What?" William said.

"During the chaos you created down in the Depository"—she grinned proudly—"I took Abraham from the cryogenic chamber. Right under their noses." She stood up. "That was the plan all along, but the chaos down there made it even easier to zap in there and grab him."

"Abraham Talley?" William blurted out.

"Yes," she said.

William sat there in disbelief. Was she telling the truth? Had she really managed to free Abraham?

"And now I'm going to send him through the Crypto Portal." She aimed the hand at William. "I'll say hello to him for you. Good-bye, you little rat!"

The high-pitched sound from her hand grew stronger, along with a deafening beeping sound that was so loud William thought his ears would explode.

He flung himself sideways as his bed was pulverized by a bright beam.

He slammed into a cabinet full of medical equipment, which fell over and crashed to the floor. Boxes of bandages and rolls of gauze rained down on him.

Another ray hit the cabinet, and it disappeared in a flash of light. Without thinking, William threw himself forward and rolled under the curtains around Pontus Dippel's bed. He glanced up and saw the old man. His eyes were closed. He had an oxygen mask over his face. His chest moved in time with the rhythmic puffs from the breathing machine. William took cover behind the bed as the woman's squeaking footsteps came closer. He could see the room through the narrow gap between the curtains. Smoke rose from the smoldering pile of metal, the only thing left of the bed he'd been lying in moments before

"Only babies and cowards hide," he heard her say as her steps came to a halt right outside the curtain. "You should come out and face me. Preserve whatever dignity you have left."

Pontus moaned and stirred. William looked up as the old man blinked his eyes and slowly opened them.

*No, not now,* William thought as Dippel reached for the mask and pulled it away. The old man looked down at William, who put his finger to his mouth, then pointed at the curtains.

William could hear the loud beeping from the woman's mechanical hand as she charged it to fire again. Then the curtains were flung to the side, and she appeared. Her wild eyes found the old man, and she grinned.

"So that's where you've been hiding, Pontus." She raised her mechanical hand. "This is almost too perfect. Two flies in one big bang."

The old man gasped and threw up his hands. "No, not again," he moaned.

Without hesitation, William grabbed hold of Pontus's gown and pulled him off the bed. He landed heavily on the floor. William tried not to panic and looked around. The door was too far away to reach in time.

"Sayonara," the woman said as her lips contorted into a wicked grin. The beeping from her hand increased. William knew that it would fire any moment now.

Desperately he scanned his surroundings for something . . . anything he could use to save himself and the old man from the deadly ray that was only seconds away from pulverizing them. His eyes stopped on the leather bag on the floor a short distance away. The cockroach peeked up from the open zipper. William had an idea. It was a long shot, but it might just work.

Then it was as if time slowed down, and everything happened in slow motion.

William placed his feet on the wall behind him, pushed away as hard as he could, and shot forward. He hit the bed, which crashed into the woman, causing her to stumble backward. William rolled across the floor, past the woman, and threw himself toward the leather bag. In one fluid motion, he grabbed the bag and hurled it toward the windows.

"NOOOOOOOO . . . ," the woman screamed.

The bag hurtled through the room and hit one of the big windows with tremendous force. The pane of glass exploded in a cloud of shards, and the orb flew out the window. The woman lunged forward, grabbing the bag in midair, clutching it like it was the most precious thing in the world. With a loud zap, she and the bag were gone.

William lay still, listening, his eyes fixed on the broken window. He expected the woman to reappear, but nothing happened. All he could hear was the wailing of an alarm out in the hallway.

Slowly he got to his feet and stood still, waiting. He didn't know what he was waiting for, but he stood still a little longer. Just to be sure. He looked down at himself to check if he was all there. He couldn't believe he'd survived.

William turned just as the door was flung open, and a herd of guard-bots rushed through the door, passivators ready.

The guard-bots surrounded William.

Then the two chauffeurs marched into the ward with Goffman right behind them. He stopped and looked at the destruction in the room, then at William.

"I can't leave you alone for a second," he said, shaking his head.

"It was her." The old man pulled himself up from behind the bed. "It was Cornelia Strangler."

"And she took him," William said. "She took Abraham from the cryogenic chamber."

Goffman's jaw dropped.

# 22

**Benjamin's hovercart raced down one of the narrow hallways** deep below the Institute. Benjamin was behind the wheel, and Goffman sat next to him.

William sat in the backseat and held on for dear life. He had never thought that the hovercart could travel this fast. He was still wearing his hospital gown. The suction from the propeller behind William made his hair flutter. He cast a quick look over his shoulder at the dozen guard-bots that were following them. Each one had a passivator in its mechanical hand.

"I checked the status in the chamber an hour ago," Benjamin shouted over the noise from the fan. "Everything was fine then."

"Could it have happened after that?" Goffman shouted back.

"The system reports no break-in. I can't see how anyone could get in there, let alone leave with a whole cryogenic container undetected." Benjamin turned the steering wheel hard, and the hovercart skidded into another hallway.

"That woman did it when everyone was down at the Depository," William shouted. But the noise from the fan drowned out his voice. He hoped that the woman had been bluffing when she told him that she had freed Abraham, but he had a sinking feeling that it was true.

The hovercart came to a screeching halt at the end of the hall. Benjamin jumped out and stopped in front of something that looked like a door you would find at Fort Knox.

"Let's get it open," Benjamin said, and placed his forehead on a scanner next to the door.

Goffman stopped in front of another scanner on the other side of the door. He leaned in and placed his forehead on it. A faint humming sound came from deep inside the wall, and a lamp over the door changed from red to green.

Benjamin backed up as the iron door started to slide open. The guard-bots gathered in formation, and everyone held their breath. A frosty mist welled out from the room on the other side and snaked toward them like a gray, enchanted carpet.

As soon as the door was open enough to squeeze inside, Benjamin leaped in.

"Wait," Goffman yelled.

But Benjamin was gone.

"Get in there." Goffman waved at the guard-bots. "Hurry!"

The guard-bots poured forward and disappeared inside one after another.

William looked at Goffman, who remained outside. It was like he was afraid to go in . . . afraid of what might be in there . . . or worse, what wouldn't.

William couldn't stand it anymore. He jumped off the hovercart and started toward the door.

He stopped as he entered the room. It was much colder in here. The room was smaller than he had imagined. He counted ten coffinlike freezers along the walls. They looked exactly like the one he'd seen under the golden ring in his visions.

Benjamin was standing in front of an empty spot in between the rows of freezers. He stood there, staring at the empty space. His breath formed puffs of gray frost. The guard-bots stood in a row behind him. Their passivators raised.

"He's gone," Benjamin said without moving. "I can't believe it. . . . He's gone."

# 23

Ten minutes later William sat across from Goffman in the back of the Institute's Rolls Royce. The chauffeurs were in the front seat as usual.

They were moving through the night at tremendous speed. It was pitch-black outside. Benjamin had stayed behind at the Institute to keep monitoring the sound waves.

William glanced at Goffman, who was digging around in a briefcase on his lap.

Pontus Dippel was sitting next to Goffman. Even though it wasn't long since he had woken up from his artificial coma, he had insisted on coming with them.

Goffman continued to rummage through his briefcase. He seemed completely beside himself. Abraham's escape had hit him hard.

"Where are we going?" William asked.

"The Institute has a secret airfield outside the city," Goffman said. "A plane will meet us there. It's going to take us to the Himalayas."

"The Himalayas?" William said, startled.

"Yes," Goffman said, and glanced up at William. "That's where the portal is, according to Benjamin's coordinates." He looked down at the odd watch he was wearing on his wrist. "Eight hours and thirty-seven minutes until he thaws," he mumbled to himself.

"Who thaws?" William asked. "Abraham?"

Goffman seemed trapped in his own thoughts. He kept rummaging through his briefcase and didn't respond.

"What is that?" William asked, pointing to the device Goffman wore on his wrist.

"It's a cryogenic monitor," Pontus Dippel said in a raspy voice. "It's linked to Abraham's freezer unit. It gives different data on the freezer. How cold it is and such."

Pontus leaned over and extended his hand.

"I'm sorry," he said, and smiled. "I don't believe we've been properly introduced."

They shook. The old man's hand felt cold.

"Pontus Dippel," Pontus said. "Curator for the Depository for Impossible Archaeology."

"I know," William said. "I saw you when you were stuck in the stone."

"That's right," the old man said. "I was lucky. She didn't mean for me to survive. But she was in a hurry. All she cared about was that old orb." Pontus paused for a bit and looked at William. "And thanks for saving me in the infirmary."

"It was instinct," William said.

Pontus turned to Goffman. "Did you find it?"

"Here it is." Goffman pulled a faded folder from the briefcase and handed it to William.

William took the folder and read what it said on the typewritten label on the front.

"Cornelia Strangler?" he read out loud.

"She died many years ago," Pontus mumbled. "But somehow she has returned from the dead."

"It wasn't until Pontus woke up and confirmed who she was that things started to fall into place." Goffman pointed his bony finger at the folder. "Look inside."

William opened it and jumped when he saw the picture on the first page.

It was an old black-and-white photograph of a woman. He recognized her immediately. It was her. The same woman who'd come to find him outside his school in Norway and at the Institute. And the person who had attacked him in the infirmary.

"That's Cornelia Strangler," Goffman said.

William couldn't take his eyes off the photo. Her gaze was hypnotic.

"You remember how Abraham Talley was discovered down in the tunnels. After he had stumbled upon that lump of luridium?"

William nodded.

"He was transported to the hospital," Goffman said, "where he disappeared without a trace a few hours later. It turns out that Cornelia Strangler took him in. Abraham was weak, and she tended him until he was better."

"Why did she help him like that?" William asked. "Didn't she know that he was a murderer?"

"Strangler isn't her real name. She changed it from something else . . . ," Pontus said. "Her real last name is . . . Talley."

William gasped.

"She's his daughter," Goffman said.

William's mouth dropped open. He didn't know what to say.

"But the real kicker is," Pontus said, "that she died, an old woman, in the mid 1900s." Pontus fell silent. Like he wanted to give William some time to process the information.

"And she has remained dead," Goffman said, "until she showed up now, at the Institute. And she seems to have reversed her age."

William looked down at the photo again.

"How is that possible?" he asked.

"We don't know," Goffman said, shrugging. "It's a mystery."

"Abraham stopped aging when he got the luridium in him," William said. "Could the same have happened to her?"

"No," Pontus said. "She doesn't show any signs of harboring luridium. Not in the amounts that would slow down aging."

"For that to happen," Goffman said, "she would need to be almost a hundred percent luridium. Like Abraham."

"And now she's managed to get away with the entire cryonic storage unit. Including the cooling elements, nitrogen container, and Abraham Talley inside." Pontus wiped his nose with a handkerchief and glanced over at Goffman.

"How?" William said.

"That mechanical hand of hers must have a very powerful defragmentation drive." Goffman paused for a bit. "It enables her to rip the atoms in any material object apart and reassemble them again in a different place."

"In simpler words," Pontus said, "it's a portable teleportation device. That's what she shot me with in the Depository."

"I'm sorry we had to keep you in the dark. And that I tried to convince you that you were hallucinating," Goffman said. "You stumbled upon Pontus when we were preparing to free him. We wanted to wait until Benjamin had found the reason for your attacks before we told you what we knew. That's why we moved Pontus to a different defragmentation laboratory."

Goffman paused.

They sat in silence for a while. William looked out the window. It was dawning on him that he had helped Cornelia activate the Crypto Portal and free Abraham from the Institute.

"So, Abraham is on the loose again," William said.

"In a way," Goffman said, glancing down at his watch. "But he's still frozen."

"For however long that lasts." Pontus shot Goffman a quick glance.

"Cornelia used you to activate the portal," Goffman said. "And now you're the only one who can deactivate it again. We have to get to the portal in the Himalayas and stop her before she manages to send Abraham through it."

"How are we going to do that?" William said.

"There will be a full briefing on the plane." Goffman leaned over and tapped his cane on the glass.

William was pushed back in his seat as the car picked up speed.

# 24

**The Rolls Royce pulled up at a set of large gates that opened,** allowing the car through and onto a large runway. The only light source was the car's headlights.

The car came to a halt, and Goffman opened the door.

"Let's go," he said, and stepped out. "The plane will be here any moment."

"Good luck." Pontus stayed seated.

"You're not coming?" William asked.

"I wish I could," the old man said. "But my health isn't what it used to be. And I've been stuck in a hunk of metal for three days."

William gave the old man a reassuring smile before he climbed out and closed the door behind him. He watched as the car drove off.

"It can drive by itself?" William asked Goffman as the car disappeared into the darkness.

"Of course," Goffman said.

"But then you don't need the chauffeurs," William said.

"Not for driving." Goffman smiled. "But they like it in the front, and they come in handy for so many other things."

The two chauffeurs positioned themselves out on the airstrip. One of them turned on a flashlight. The beam of light pointed up into the starlit night.

William and Goffman watched the sky, but every now and then Goffman would glance at the cryogenic monitor strapped to his wrist.

Finally there was a distant hum.

"Here they come," Goffman said, pointing to the sky.

A gigantic airplane materialized in the black sky above them, approaching at high speed.

"Where's it going to land?" William asked.

"It's not," Goffman replied.

William stood spellbound, staring at the huge plane. It stopped in the air above them and hung there. The plane had to be as long as a football field. It was shaped like an enormous whale, was white as snow, and had no windows. Not even in the front, where the pilots would usually sit on a regular airplane. A hatch opened in the bottom of the plane, and a platform lowered itself, finally stopping in front of them.

"Come on," Goffman said, stepping onto it.

Soon William, Goffman, and the two chauffeurs were standing in a large cargo hold inside the plane. The hatch in the floor closed behind them, and the humming of the powerful engines grew louder as the plane began to accelerate.

"The plane will take us to the Himalayas," Goffman said. "We're prepared for most eventualities. That device over there, for example, is a snowmobile."

Goffman pointed to a machine the size of a small tractor with belts instead of wheels and an enclosed cabin on top.

"And those are escape pods over there," Goffman said, pointing to two glass spheres sitting in front of a large door in the wall.

"What for?" William asked.

"In case anything should happen," Goffman said.

"Glass escape pods?" William said. "That seems like a strange material choice."

"Shatter-resistant glass," Goffman said.

"And those over there?" William asked, pointing to a row of gray jumpsuits hanging along the wall.

"The latest prototype of our ultrasuits. We're very proud of this model," Goffman said.

William walked over to one of the suits. "What do they do?" he asked.

"They're made of material that changes attributes

depending on the circumstances," Goffman said. "And the soles on the bottoms of the boots adapt to the surface you're walking on."

William ran his fingers over the material. He could feel it changing texture as he touched it.

"Cool," he whispered to himself. "It's as if it's alive."

"Welcome, Mr. Goffman," a voice said from behind them.

William turned around and saw a square robot the size of a milk crate. It looked up at them with a big, ball-like eye.

"I'll show you to your rooms. The briefing is in T minus thirty-one minutes," the strange crate-shaped robot continued. "Follow me."

Goffman and William followed the robot as it hobbled away.

"Now that I have you here . . ." The robot looked up at Goffman with its big eye. "There are a couple of things I'd like to discuss with you."

"Okay?" Goffman said.

"I need a real name. I'm tired of not having a name," the crate said. "And I'm tired of all the nicknames: Boxer, Square-Pants, Crate, et cetera."

"For the time being, we'll call you Beta. That will have to do. You haven't even been patented yet," Goffman said. "And you're still not completely done."

"If I might suggest a change, it would have to be my shape," Beta said. "Round might be more practical. Then I could roll instead of thumping along. And I would get cool nicknames like Bounce, Globe, or Speed-Ball."

"We'll see," Goffman said, and then turned to William. "You have your own compartment. I recommend that you get a little sleep. We'll hold a briefing on the situation soon. Beta will show you the way."

"Follow me," Beta said, clattering away across the metal floor like a clumsy die.

William stepped into a spacious compartment and looked around. There was a bed, a small sofa, and a desk. A flat-screen TV on the wall was displaying a picture of clouds and blue sky.

William walked over to the screen and studied it.

"This plane doesn't have windows, so each room has a screen that shows you what's going on outside," Beta said. "Not being able to see out causes some people claustrophobia. The screens help."

"Cool," William said.

"It gets cooler. In five minutes we'll leave the atmosphere and enter space."

"Space?" William asked, staring at the robot.

"Yup," Beta said. "We travel a lot faster without the air resistance, like traveling in a vacuum. Conventional planes take twelve hours. We'll be there in a little under two."

"Wow," William said, impressed.

"There'll be a briefing in the canteen in approximately thirty minutes," Beta informed him, and backed out of the room.

William sat on the bed. He felt drained. A million thoughts whizzed through his head. It felt like a bad dream. . . . Abraham was on the loose again, and now they were chasing after him to the Himalayas.

William put his face in his hands. How could he have been so stupid to be tricked into solving the orb?

He promised himself that from now on he was going to be more alert. More vigilant. If he was the reason for the mess they were in, he would have to be the one to get them out of it.

# 25

**Thirty minutes later William jogged down a narrow hallway** behind the square robot, which clunked to a halt outside a white door.

The door opened with a soft swoosh, and they continued inside.

William stopped as the door closed behind him. They were in the plane's canteen. A row of five large tables stood in front of them.

A small group of people was gathered around the table at the end of the room. Goffman waved at William, who walked over and stopped.

"Now we're all here." Goffman pointed to two people already seated at the table with their backs to William.

Iscia turned around and smiled at him.

"Iscia!" William hadn't seen her since the disaster at the Depository of Impossible Archaeology. She seemed fine. At last there was some good news. "What are you doing here?" he asked with a surprised smile.

"What do you think?" she said, and smiled back. "We're here to help."

"We?" William asked, glancing at the person sitting next to her.

Freddy turned around and looked at him.

William stood still for a moment, a mixture of feelings bubbling up within him. On one hand, he was glad Iscia was here. On the other . . . Freddy.

"Come have a seat," Goffman said, gesturing for William to sit down.

William walked over to the only free seat, right next to Freddy. He hesitated.

Freddy stood up and held out his hand.

"William, it's so nice to see you," he said.

"Uh . . . ?" was all William managed to say.

Freddy stood there smiling with his hand outstretched.

"Shake his hand, already!" Iscia whispered loudly.

William took Freddy's hand, and they shook.

"Have a seat," Freddy said, pulling the chair out for him.

William sat.

Goffman pulled a remote control out of his pocket and pushed one of the buttons. A hologram of a golden ring appeared in the air right above the tabletop and began to rotate slowly. It was covered with strange symbols. William recognized it right away. It was the same golden ring he'd seen during his attacks.

Goffman pointed at the rotating ring. "We have deciphered hundreds of pages of coded text found in ancient documents from all over the word. And to our knowledge, this is very close to what the Crypto Portal looks like."

Goffman paused, took a sip of water from a glass on the table, cleared his throat, and continued. "Up until today, we thought that the Crypto Portal had been destroyed thousands of years ago. That was until William solved the orb at the Depository of Impossible Archaeology and remotely brought the portal back to life somehow."

"What does the portal do?" William asked. "Where does it lead?"

Goffman scratched his chin as he watched the rotating hologram. "We don't know that much about the portal." He cleared his throat. "But, according to the texts, it was used to evacuate humankind from the earth a long time ago and, with it, luridium."

"How long ago?" William asked.

"From what we've been able to decipher," Goffman said, "it happened right before the Karoo Ice Age, which started around three hundred sixty million years ago."

William sat up in his seat, startled.

"There weren't people on earth that long ago," he blurted out.

"Not according to mainstream science," Goffman said. "But the three of you have seen all the impossible objects at the Depository. And we know from the texts that intelligent, humanlike beings made the portal before the Karoo Ice Age."

"Which means that it's older than three hundred sixty million years?" Iscia said.

Goffman nodded.

"But how is the portal connected to what has been happening at the Institute?" Iscia asked.

"Cornelia stole Abraham from the cryogenic chamber," Goffman said. "It would appear that she plans to send him through the portal when he thaws."

"But isn't that a good thing?" Freddy asked. "If she sends him away, we won't have to worry about him anymore."

"I wish it were that simple, Freddy," Goffman said. He almost smiled. "Ever since Abraham's body was invaded by luridium, we believe he's been working to get luridium back to earth. We think this behavior is programmed into the metal itself, making Abraham act on *behalf* of the luridium."

"Programmed," William said. "How?"

Goffman paused and took another sip of water. "When the luridium enters a living body, the information programmed into it invades the brain of the infected and takes over. Simply put, it's like transferring data."

"A form of mind control?" William gasped.

"Yes," Goffman said with a quick nod. "We call it stealth mind control, since the victim is unaware of being controlled. The programmed information comes across as one's own thoughts."

"But why doesn't the luridium control William in the same way?" Iscia asked, looking over at William.

"It appears that William has a higher resistance," Goffman said. "Instead, the luridium makes his innate code-breaking talent stronger. Your grandfather knew the risks when he injected the luridium into you. And that's why he made sure to inject you with only forty-nine percent luridium. If he had gone over that, you might be a very different boy now."

"So," Iscia continued. "There's no danger of this happening to William?"

Goffman swallowed and looked at William. "There's always a danger. But we think that if it hasn't happened by now, it probably won't." Goffman looked at William. "Because of your natural resistance, I think that if you happened to absorb more luridium into your body, it would only enhance your abilities. However, that's speculation; we can't be sure."

Iscia folded her arms over her chest and sat back in her

chair. She shot William a concerned look like she didn't fully buy Goffman's explanation.

"Where does the portal lead?" William asked. He wanted to take the focus off himself.

"We don't know for sure and can only guess," Goffman said. "But according to the texts . . . it leads to a different dimension."

"She's going to send Abraham to a different dimension?" Freddy sounded stunned.

"I think that's her plan," Goffman replied.

"But why?" Iscia asked.

"According to the information the Institute has gathered . . ." Goffman cleared his throat again. "A long time ago there were intelligent beings on earth who invented luridium."

"Humans?" Iscia shot in.

"Yes, humans," Goffman said, and scratched his chin nervously. "But the luridium turned against them and took over their bodies, then used the portal to evacuate earth right before a great ice age hit."

"How did they evacuate?" William said.

"It used the human bodies as vessels," Goffman said. "It can only move around via someone's body. A human . . . or an animal. We think that the luridium left earth because it had destroyed almost all life here. And it went looking for new life-forms out there to invade and conquer."

"That's luridium's main goal?" Iscia asked. "To invade and conquer?"

Goffman nodded.

"The only thing that makes luridium weaker is extreme cold. So we believe that was another reason for it to leave before the ice age."

"That also explains why Abraham was cryogenically frozen at the Institute," William said.

"Correct," Goffman said. "The cold temporarily shuts down his powers, and he is too weak to do anything. As soon as he thaws, his powers will be restored, and he will be strong enough to make the transition through the portal."

"But what happens if he's sent through?" Iscia asked.

"We can't know for sure," Goffman said. His face twitched nervously. "But we can't take any chances. We know that Abraham wants to bring the luridium back to earth to finish the job of infecting all the people here. And . . ." Goffman stopped for a moment, his eyes staring blankly in front of him.

"And?" William said.

Goffman snapped back into the present and looked at William. "And in the worst case, the luridium will return. And if that happens, humankind, in fact all life on this planet, is doomed."

"So we have to stop Cornelia from sending him through the portal," William said.

"Correct." Goffman looked at William. "And you're the only one who has the code-breaking skills to do it."

William nodded. He would do whatever he had to do to stop Cornelia.

"The only problem," Goffman continued, "is that we don't know how William will respond when he's that close to the portal—especially if that *is* what has been causing his attacks. And we believe it is"

William felt as though he had been zapped with electricity.

"That's what has been causing my attacks?" he asked.

"Yes," Goffman said. "Benjamin got a clear reading when you solved the orb at the Depository. The portal emits powerful sound waves that radiate across the globe and provoke your attacks."

"So every time I've had an attack, it was because of the Crypto Portal?" William asked.

Goffman nodded. "It seems Cornelia has been trying to activate it, and that's what has triggered your attacks."

"But why does the portal affect him?" Iscia asked.

"It has been dormant for years and hasn't been sending out any signals," Goffman said. "But since Cornelia stole the orb from the Depository, she's been trying to activate it, and she has been partially successful. When that occurs, the portal starts emitting bursts of signals. Since you are still more human than luridium," Goffman said, looking directly at William, "it causes these attacks. The same thing happened to the cockroach Benjamin had in his lab."

"So what do we do when we get to the Himalayas?" William asked.

"Your grandfather has been there since he dropped you off," Goffman replied.

"He has?" William almost shouted.

"Yes," Goffman said, smiling for the first time in a while. "Benjamin has been guiding him and trying to locate the source of the signals. It's been a struggle. But when you solved the orb at the Depository, they pinpointed the source of the signals. Your grandfather found the entrance to an ancient underground system in the mountains. We will meet up with him when we get there and try to close the portal."

William felt a sudden surge of relief. So that's what his grandfather had been doing. Now he understood why his grandfather had to rush away. It wasn't because he didn't care about William. It was because he had much more serious matters to take care of.

Goffman gave William a serious look. "We'll get you to the Himalayas and meet your grandfather there. Your grandfather will take us down into the system where the portal is, but you're the only one who can deactivate it. Cornelia will stop at nothing to prevent you from interfering." Goffman paused. "Do you think you can handle it?"

William nodded.

He had to handle it.

He had to.

# 26

**Only when William was back in his quarters did the** overwhelming terror set in.

It hit him that he was going to the Himalayas, where Cornelia Strangler and the person he feared most in his life, Abraham Talley, were waiting. And only he could prevent Cornelia from sending Abraham through the Crypto Portal. The same portal that caused his severe attacks and made him lose control over his own body.

The task seemed impossible.

His eyes were drawn to the flat-screen on the wall. The image was gradually going from black to blue. The plane must be descending, leaving space.

There was a sudden knock on the door. It opened, and Iscia poked her head in.

"Are you busy?" she asked.

"No," William said, and got up. "Come inside." He was glad to see her.

"You got a bigger room than me," Iscia said, sitting down on his bed. She rocked back and forth, as if testing the mattress. "A nicer bed, too."

William didn't know what to say. How could she be talking about rooms and beds at a time like this?

"I like this plane," Iscia said, smiling. "Too bad we won't be on it longer."

They sat gazing around the room for a few seconds.

"How are you doing?" she asked, glancing at him.

"Fine," he lied.

"You almost destroyed the entire Depository at the Institute," Iscia said. "I can't believe they didn't send you straight home."

"Goffman wasn't as mad as I thought he would be," William said.

"That's because he has his hands full right now," Iscia said.

William nodded.

"Plus . . . he needs your skills."

The plane shook, and Iscia held on to the bed.

"Turbulence." William looked toward the flat-screen on the wall. It showed a wide mountain chain far below them. That must mean they were approaching the Himalayas.

"It's beautiful," Iscia said. "Have you been here before?"

"No." William shook his head. "You?"

"Never, but I've always wanted to go."

Iscia grabbed the bed and held on as the plane shook again.

"I hate turbulence," she said, looking toward the TV. "The weather seems fine. Why are we bouncing around like this?"

"There can be turbulence in nice weather too," William explained, "but it's harmless."

They sat for a little while in silence. The plane continued to vibrate. It felt like they were sliding down a snowy hill on a large sled.

"Where's Freddy?" William asked.

"In his room," Iscia replied. "He said he had a headache. He's been acting a little strange ever since that business in the Depository."

"Strange?" William said. "How?"

"Don't know really . . . just strange." She looked at William. "What do you make of all that stuff Goffman told us?"

"It's a scary story," William said.

"Yeah." Iscia shrugged. "It made me think of an old roll of parchment down in the Depository. The text talks about an advanced civilization disappearing from earth millions of years ago." She shot him an inquisitive look. "Could that have been the same civilization Goffman was talking about?"

Now it was William's turn to shrug.

"It could be. If there was an advanced civilization on earth before us, and they invented something so intelligent . . . like luridium . . . and it turned on them . . . took over their bodies . . ." William paused. It was a scary thought.

"Almost like where our own civilization is now," Iscia said. "With robots and all that advanced technology."

"Yeah," William said.

The plane shook as they hit more turbulence.

"Don't you feel relieved?" Iscia asked.

"What do you mean?" William asked, giving her a quizzical look.

"That they found out what's been triggering your attacks?"

"In a way," he said, fidgeting.

"In a way?" she asked.

"We're on our way to the source of the attacks right now," William responded, looking at his hands.

Iscia's face grew serious. She was about to say something but was interrupted as the plane shook again. This time it didn't stop. The shaking only increased, and an alarm started wailing from somewhere out in the hallway.

"What's going on?" Iscia cried, scrambling to her feet.

William staggered toward the door, which Iscia had already opened so she could peer out into the corridor.

"Nothing to worry about, a little mild turbulence," a flat voice stated.

William looked down and saw Beta on its way past the door.

"This is more than turbulence," William said.

"Well, there's also a slight problem with the electrical system on the plane," Beta said.

"What problem?" William asked.

The floor disappeared underneath them as they were flung up against the ceiling. William grabbed hold with his hands and hung on.

"Nothing to worry about," Beta said. "Only a little free fall."

"Free fall?" William yelled back.

"Yes . . . a little," Beta said. "It'll be over soon."

"What will be over? Our lives?" Iscia shouted. She was pressed up against the ceiling right next to William.

"Look," Iscia shouted, and pointed at something below them. "What's that?"

William looked down and saw a spiderlike thing jumping out from a small door in the wall. A sign on the door read FUSE BOX. There was a loud electrical crackle from the fuse box; then sparks flew out as if a firecracker had exploded inside.

The spider-thing landed on the floor and scurried down the hallway below them. At first William thought it was some kind of robot. But as it passed under them, he recognized it: It was Cornelia Strangler's mechanical hand. Her hand could move around on its own.

"She's on the plane," William shouted. "Cornelia's behind this." He watched as the hand sped down the hallway and disappeared around a corner.

The plane shook again, and they crashed to the floor.

"We have to find the others," William cried as he got to his feet and grabbed Iscia's hand. "This way," he yelled, pulling her down the hallway.

The plane shook again, and the lights went out.

"I can't see anything," Iscia shouted over the noise from the screaming engines.

"Emergency power generator activated," Beta said from right behind them.

A red light came on in the ceiling.

"Beta! Where are the others?" Iscia asked.

"One moment," Beta said.

William and Iscia staggered down the hallway and stopped at a door. A sign on it said TO THE ESCAPE PODS in big green letters. Iscia pushed on the door, but it was locked.

"The others are on their way to the escape pods," Beta said. "You should go there too. The plane's autopilot is flying, and we'll be making an uncontrolled, controlled emergency landing."

*"Uncontrolled . . . ?"* William shot Beta a startled look. "You told me there was nothing to worry about!"

"Would you care for a little calming music to soothe the nerves?" Beta asked.

"While we're waiting to crash?" William shouted.

Pleasant piano music poured out of a little speaker on the front of the cube-shaped robot. Iscia looked at William, her eyes wide with fear.

"Beta . . . the door is locked. Can you open it?" William struggled to be heard over the deafening noise and piano music. The plane shuddered so violently now that it was almost impossible for them to stay upright.

"One moment," Beta said.

Then the body of the plane trembled and tilted forward. It felt like the nose was pointing straight down. The walls around them shook so much that William was afraid the whole plane would come apart at any moment. The drone of the engines increased even more. Iscia was still clinging to the door handle.

The door opened with a click.

William and Iscia rushed through it and almost fell down the stairs. The robot followed them while counting down.

"Uncontrolled, controlled emergency landing in T minus three minutes," it said.

"This way," Iscia yelled, pointing to an open door.

William felt the wind rush at them.

"They're not leaving us behind," William called back, "are they?"

"Uncontrolled, controlled emergency landing in T minus two and a half minutes," Beta announced.

They fought their way into the cargo hold where the two escape pods were.

"It's open," Iscia shouted, and pointed at the escape hatch at the other end of the large room.

William spotted Goffman, Freddy, and a chauffeur next to the two escape pods by the escape hatch. All three of them were struggling to get into their ultrasuits. Goffman's face filled with relief when he spotted William and Iscia.

"You made it," he shouted. "One of the chauffeurs is looking for you. Hurry up and put on the suits! We have to get into the escape pod before the plane hits the ground." Goffman took down two ultrasuits and tossed them to William and Iscia.

The plane shook again, and the escape pods swayed.

"Uncontrolled, controlled emergency landing in T minus two minutes," Beta said, bobbing in through the door and filling the room with soothing piano music.

William fought to get his suit on. It wasn't easy, almost like putting on a wet suit.

The second chauffeur came in through the door and

helped to prepare the escape pods. Goffman got in, and Freddy jumped after him. William hadn't managed to get his ultrasuit all the way on yet. He hobbled toward the pod.

"Come on!" William shouted, waving at Iscia, who was also still struggling with her own suit.

"Uncontrolled, controlled emergency landing in T minus one minute," Beta said.

"Get in here now!" Goffman waved, sticking his head out of the pod's door.

William grabbed Iscia and pulled her along. There was another boom, and the plane shook so violently they both fell.

When William looked up again, he saw that the escape pod with Goffman and the others inside had broken free. It was on its way out the open doorway.

"No, wait!" he shouted.

"Look out!" Iscia pointed at something. "Behind you."

William threw himself to the side as the snowmobile skidded toward the door and crashed into the escape pod. William got to his feet and saw Goffman's terror-stricken face staring back at him as the escape pod and snowmobile tumbled into the snowy chaos outside the plane.

"Uncontrolled, controlled emergency landing in T minus ten seconds," Beta said. "Nine . . . eight . . . seven . . ."

"We have to take the other one!" William shouted.

They got to their feet. Iscia took his hand, and William

used the last of his strength for the short sprint to the pod. He pulled the glass door open and jumped inside, dragging Iscia in after him.

The round pod had ten seats along the wall and a red lever sticking up from the floor. William threw himself into a seat, and a seat belt shot out, securing him.

Once Iscia was strapped in beside him, William pulled on the lever. The escape pod rolled toward the door. He cast one last look back as they bounced out into the storm.

A figure was standing in the room they had left: It was Cornelia.

She grinned at him as her mechanical hand scurried toward her across the floor. It jumped through the air. She caught it and screwed it back into place at the end of her arm. She waved at him.

"Have a nice death," her voice said from inside William's head.

And with a burst of light, she was gone.

# 27

*Stop it,* William thought.

He wiped his face, trying to brush away whatever was stinging him. A wave of intense cold poured through his body, and he tried opening his eyes. But it was like they were frozen shut.

When he finally managed to force them open, all he could see was white.

He was lying in the middle of an endless ocean of snow. The wind howled around him and whipped more snow into his face. He couldn't see farther than a few yards. He looked at his fingers: They were white with frostbite. He had to get out of the cold before it was too late, had to start moving, try to warm up again. After struggling up onto his knees, he looked around for any sign of the others or the plane . : . or anything.

But he saw nothing.

William put his hands over his face and blew into them to try to warm up his cheeks, which were frozen stiff. But he was so cold that the air coming out of his mouth felt like ice.

Slowly he felt warmth spreading through his body. He looked down and realized that the heat was coming from the ultrasuit he was wearing. A small red light on the chest was blinking, and he could feel his strength returning.

He raised one arm and watched as a glove grew out of the sleeve and covered his hand. Then he felt something rising upward from the collar of his suit. In a flash a warm hood had formed around his head. Now only his face was exposed.

His breathing calmed down, and he stood up. The wind was still howling around him. But now that he was warming up, he could think clearly.

He had to find the others, so he started walking.

"ISCIAAAAA!" he shouted.

But his voice was drowned out by the howling wind, which seemed to be increasing in strength. William kept moving through the deep snow. It reached up to his waist, and he had to use his arms to dig his way forward. He stopped and looked around in despair. That's when he spotted something a little way away. Something round in the snow in front of him. He squinted into the wind.

It was the escape pod.

William fought his way over to the glass orb and looked inside.

It was empty.

He scanned his surroundings.

"IIIIISCIIIIIAAAAAA!" William shouted again. If Iscia had left the pod and started walking, the wind and blowing snow would have covered her tracks immediately.

William looked at the pod. What should he do? Seek shelter inside and wait for help? What if Iscia was trapped out there in the storm? Or lying somewhere, unconscious and freezing to death?

He had to keep going. He had to look for Iscia.

And that's when he saw it: a red light blinking in the distance. It pulsated with three short, three long, and three short bursts. William knew what that meant. It was an SOS. The international code for distress. Someone needed help.

It was difficult to judge how far away the beacon was. William peered down at the light on his chest. It blinked in the same rhythm.

There was someone there. In the storm. Someone with an ultrasuit like his.

It had to be Iscia or one of the others from the plane.

Then the light disappeared.

William stared into the white, fixing his gaze on the spot where the light had been, hoping that it would return, but it didn't.

He started walking, fighting his way through the waist-deep snow. He couldn't stop now. He had to keep moving in the direction where the light had been. Even if every step was a struggle as his legs sank into the snow, he had to find the light.

He caught a glimpse of something in all the whiteness ahead of him.

A dark fleck.

He sped up. Was it the plane? Or a person?

As he moved closer, the contours of a mountain appeared before him. He realized that the dark fleck ahead of him was the entrance to a cave. Was that where the light had come from?

He kept going.

Soon he was standing at the entrance, peering into the darkness of the cave. Snow covered the area around the entrance. But farther in the ground was bare. William took a couple of steps forward, then stopped and listened. The only thing he could hear was the howling wind behind him.

"Hello?"

But the only response was his own echo.

He continued deeper into the dark cave. Water dripped from the roof, and as he moved farther, it became increasingly difficult to see. He considered turning around and heading back out.

A beam of light shot out from the top of his head. It seemed the ultrasuit had a built-in automatic flashlight. The narrow beam gave out enough light to see details in the darkness in front of him.

"Hello?" he called again as he walked.

The howling from the storm outside grew quieter. The floor of the cave was slick and wet. He could feel the soles of his boots changing with each step. It felt like his feet were being sucked to the ground to give him a firm footing.

William stopped as the red light reappeared in the darkness in front of him. It blinked in the same rhythm it had done before. Three short, three long, three short. SOS.

"Is anyone there?" William asked.

But there was no reply.

He aimed his flashlight at the red light. But it was just beyond the beam's reach. He still couldn't see what the source was, so he continued on.

As he got closer, he started seeing the contours of a shape around the red light. It was a body. It seemed to be suspended in midair a couple of yards above the ground.

William stopped.

He was too far away to see who it was. He hesitated, wondering what he should do. He took a couple more tentative steps forward and pointed his light at the lifeless form that hung there as if suspended by some invisible force.

He moved closer.

And now he saw who it was.

Her eyes were closed, and her head tilted forward.

"Iscia!" he shouted, and ran toward her.

It was like he hit an invisible wall. The air in front of him crackled, and he was flung backward. William landed hard on his back on the stone ground.

He sat up, dazed.

"Iscia!" he yelled again.

But she didn't move.

"ISCIA!" William shouted at the top of his lungs.

Still no reaction.

"She can't hear you," a hoarse voice said. It seemed to come from inside his own head, and he immediately knew who it was.

He looked around and saw a dark shadow farther back in the cave.

"Cornelia," William said.

The figure didn't respond.

"What did you do to her?"

"I saved her," Cornelia said, walking into his beam of light. "You should thank me."

"Thank you? You were on the plane," he said. "You made it crash. I heard your voice in my head. You tried to kill us."

"But now you're here anyway," Cornelia said. "You're a hard one to get rid of."

She took a step closer. She bared her teeth in a sort of sneer.

"You shouldn't have come here," she said. "And now you're going to pay the price."

There was something animal-like about her eyes. She was more like a wolf than a human. Her eyes almost glowed.

William looked around for something he could use as a weapon, a rock . . . anything at all. His body tensed, preparing for battle. His fear was replaced with rage. He wasn't going to let her harm Iscia.

Cornelia walked over to the girl hanging lifeless in midair.

"Don't touch her!" William yelled. He got up and ran toward them, slamming into the invisible wall again.

For the second time he was flung backward and landed on the ground. He got to his feet and started toward Cornelia again. She raised her mechanical hand, pushed a button, and shot a beam of light, which hit him in the chest. William's body stiffened completely, and he stood there, unable to move. It was like he'd been passivized. The only difference was that he didn't fall over. It was as if an invisible force held him up. Was there no end to what she could do with that mechanical hand of hers?

Cornelia turned and walked toward William, stopping directly in front of him. She leaned in so close that her nose almost touched his. Her breath stank of burned rubber, stinging his eyes.

"Why are you doing this?" William asked. "Don't you know what Abraham is capable of?"

"Of course I know." Cornelia snickered. "I'm only finishing what my grandmother started."

"Your grandmother?" William repeated. "They said that you were his *daughter*. That you died and came back somehow."

This seemed to please Cornelia. She laughed loudly.

"Those stupid people." She chuckled. "They think I came back from the dead?"

Her laughter stopped as quickly as it had begun. She set her crazy eyes on him.

"I'm the third generation," she said. "My grandmother was his daughter. When she died, my mother took over and then me after her."

"There've been three of you?" William said, surprised.

"I'm Cornelia Strangler the Third," Cornelia said with a proud smile. "Born to serve Abraham." Her eyes flickered madly when she said Abraham's name.

Cornelia pushed her face even closer to William's. Her rancid breath made it almost impossible for him to breathe.

"I'm going to complete what my grandmother and mother set out to do," she said with a proud smile. "I'm going to send him through the portal."

"Do you realize what could happen if you do?" William asked.

"Of course," she said through clenched teeth. "The earth belongs to those who left. And now it's time for them to return, and Abraham Talley is going to bring them back."

"You're crazy," William said, gritting his teeth. He tried to wiggle free from the invisible force that was holding him, but he was stuck.

Cornelia raised her mechanical arm and held it up in front of his face.

"I could end you here and now," she said, her dry lips twisting. "Both of you."

William fought the urge to close his eyes, forced himself not to blink. He wouldn't give her the satisfaction of showing that he was afraid.

"But since you're already here with all those fools from the Institute," she said, "you might come in handy. You've got a lot of fight in you, and Abraham could use someone like that."

William blinked. What was she talking about?

She pressed her cold mechanical fist into his face.

"Here's what you're going to do," she said. "When you find the other idiots, you don't say anything about our little meeting. And when you get to the portal, you're going to help me send Abraham through it. Then you'll get to see your little girlfriend again in one piece."

Cornelia pulled back her fist and straightened up. Those piercing eyes of hers were still trained on him.

"Help you?" William said. "How?"

"By not doing anything." Cornelia grinned. "They think you're going to deactivate the portal. And you're going to pretend that you are . . . but you're NOT!"

William felt his heart sink. She had him. It was the perfect plan.

"And when they ask you where she is"—she pointed at Iscia—"you'll say you got separated in the crash. If you tell them anything about our meeting here, she's gone forever."

William knew that she had the upper hand now. She was in control, and there was nothing he could do about it.

"Okay," William whispered. He had no choice but to play along for the moment.

Cornelia turned and headed toward Iscia.

"And there's one more little thing," she said, turning back toward him.

William looked at her, dreading what was coming next.

"When Abraham is through the portal . . ." She paused. "You're going through it after him. . . . You two are made of the same stuff. That's where you belong . . . with him."

William's heart sank. This couldn't be happening. She wanted to send him through the portal with Talley?

Cornelia grinned, baring her brown teeth. "And if you screw this up, then Iscia is . . ." Cornelia pulled her finger over her own throat. "She'll remain unharmed as long as you play along."

Then she pointed to William with her mechanical hand.

The ray hit him with so much force that he was flung backward. But this time he didn't land on the rocky floor of the cave.

He was in a free fall, hurtling through the air.

# 28

**William landed heavily in the snow.**

He tried to breathe but couldn't. He was trapped. His arms moved desperately as he tried to dig his way out. Which way was up?

Someone grabbed his feet, pulling him free and setting him on the ground.

"It's William!" he heard Goffman shout.

Two strong hands helped him to his feet and urged him toward the snowmobile. It was one of the chauffeurs. William's legs trembled, and he had a problem staying upright. Goffman waved at him from the open door in the vehicle. William climbed in through the door and fell into a seat.

Goffman hopped into the seat next to him.

"We've been looking for you everywhere. We thought

you hadn't—" he began, but cut himself short. He shook his head. "Where's Iscia?"

William wanted to tell him everything—about Cornelia, Abraham, and the cave—but he couldn't. He couldn't risk anything happening to Iscia. He needed time to think.

"She's not with you?" Goffman looked startled.

"No." William sat up.

"You were with her when the plane crashed," Goffman said. "Didn't you see what happened to her?"

"I hit my head," William said. "When I came to, she was gone. So was the plane."

"The plane is equipped with a chameleon generator," Goffman said. "It activates in emergency situations and makes the plane invisible." Goffman looked out at the snow whipping the windshield. "We have to find her." He pointed at one of the two chauffeurs. "Go look for her."

The chauffeur nodded, turned, and disappeared into the white storm.

William caught Freddy's gaze. The other boy didn't look so friendly anymore. He stared at William through narrowed eyes.

"Are you sure you don't know where she is?" he asked.

"Yes," William said.

"Leave him alone, Freddy," Goffman said.

"It's weird," Freddy said. "They were together, and

then she disappeared?" Freddy leaned back in the seat and crossed his arms over his chest.

"If she's out there, the chauffeur will find her," Goffman said. "Besides, she's got an ultrasuit. It'll help her."

William hated the thought that Iscia was alone with that crazy woman.

"We have to get to the portal," Goffman said, glancing down at his cryogenic monitor. He nodded to the chauffeur behind the wheel, and the snowmobile moved off again.

Some while later, the vehicle stopped.

"This is it," Goffman said, looking at the coordinates on the GPS screen in front of him.

William looked out the window but couldn't see anything except white.

"There's nothing out there," Freddy said.

"Look up." Goffman pointed through the glass roof.

High above them was something that looked like a floating temple surrounded by white. William gasped, his eyes fixed on the building. Then he saw the contours of a mountain around it. As he raised his gaze even more, he saw the ragged edges of the top of the mountain. The temple was built in the middle of a vertical stone wall.

"According to the coordinates," Goffman said, "the entrance is through that monastery up there."

"Why did they build a monastery in the middle of a mountainside?" Freddy asked.

"It was common back then," Goffman said. "The elevation made it easier to defend against attackers."

"Do we have to climb up there?" Freddy asked.

"No," Goffman said, and waved at the chauffeur behind the wheel.

The android pressed a button, and the snowmobile shook as it rose, wobbling, from the ground. William looked out the window and saw long metal legs unfolding on both sides of the vehicle.

"It's biomimetics," Goffman explained. "We are highly inspired by nature. And a lot of our research in the Institute is biomimetics related. The exoskeletons are inspired by beetles. And we based the legs for the snowmobile on crab legs. Fasten your seat belts. This is going to get steep."

William looked out the window at the metal legs that now extended out from the vehicle. They reminded him of his own crab. The one he had made at home for his school assignment.

The whole vehicle tipped backward as the front legs grabbed hold of the rock face and started climbing, carrying them upward. The snowmobile shook as the mechanical legs lifted them higher and higher.

William peered down at the icy ground far below. He had never been fond of heights, but falling was the least of his worries now. He looked over at Freddy, who clung to the seat in front of him, fear visible in his wide eyes.

The snowmobile jerked as one of the legs lost its grip, and they tilted to the side. Freddy screamed, fell out of his seat, and slid down the aisle. He crashed into the wall at the rear of the snowmobile.

"Seat belt," Goffman shouted.

"I forgot," Freddy cried, crawling into the nearest seat.

The snowmobile regained its grip and continued the ascent up the steep mountainside.

A few nerve-racking minutes later, they reached the ledge outside the monastery and came to a halt.

"Everyone out," Goffman said. "We don't have much time." He opened the door and exited.

William got up and followed him.

The ledge where the snowmobile was parked seemed to be protected from the wind. Now William could see the monastery in every detail. It looked like a Tibetan temple. Only much older than the ones William had seen in photos of similar structures. The roof tiles were dark green, and the stone walls glimmered with something that looked like gold.

William looked at Goffman, who stood in the snow next to him. His head whipped from side to side as his eyes scanned the surroundings.

"Where is Tobias?" Goffman said, and glanced down at his wristwatch. "He said he would meet us here."

"You made it," a familiar voice said.

William turned and saw a ragged figure coming toward them down the monastery steps.

His hair and beard were scruffy, and his clothes were dirty. A passivator hung from a strap over his shoulder.

"Grandpa!" William shouted, wading through the snow toward his grandfather.

"You made it," Tobias said, lifting him into the air and swinging him around.

William clung to his grandfather as he fought back tears and the lump growing in his throat. He wanted so badly to tell him about Cornelia and her plan to send him through the portal together with Abraham. But he couldn't. Not yet.

Setting William down on the ground, his grandfather put his arm around him and pulled him toward the monastery.

"Come . . . we'll talk on the way."

The small group continued up the stairs and in through the gilded doors.

The interior was dark. The only light came from a fire in the middle of the empty hall. This monastery had clearly been abandoned a long time ago. William stopped and looked around. As his eyes adjusted to the dark, he saw hunched-over figures gathered around the fire. There were three of them, and they had large furs draped over their shoulders.

"Sherpas," his grandfather said, stopping next to

William. "They've been helping me, but they refuse to go inside. Something about an old myth."

"What myth?" William asked without taking his eyes off the Sherpas.

"That anyone who goes into the sacred caves will never return," Grandfather said, forcing a smile.

"Is this place made by the same people who made the luridium?" William said.

"This monastery is millions of years old," his grandfather said. "But the portal is even older, and I think that this monastery was built by people much more recently. They must have found the portal and thought it was a gate to the underworld. And they built all of this around it."

William nodded.

"Come," his grandfather said, moving deeper into the monastery.

Soon, they came to a halt before a round brass door. It stood ajar. William ran his fingers over the strange symbols covering it. The door was divided into smaller pieces that could be moved.

"The door is protected by codes," his grandfather said. "It took me a while, but I finally cracked them." He grabbed the door and pulled on it. The door slid open, revealing a small room on the other side.

"An elevator?" William said.

"Yes," his grandfather replied. "Isn't it amazing? Those

ancient people had a knack for technology. It gets better. Come." He stepped into the elevator and motioned for them all to follow.

The door slid shut behind them. William looked up at a glass sphere in the ceiling. It glowed green from the inside.

"Everything we know about the civilization that made this stuff," his grandfather said, "comes from old texts we have at the Institute. They called it Opal gas." He pointed at the lamp. "The gas comes from deep inside the earth. It seems to be charged by some kind of electricity. It provides most of the lighting down there. Has done for eons. I'm sure you have many questions, and I'll tell you more as we go along."

William glanced over at Freddy, who stared back at him. Iscia had been right. He was acting strange. There was a different look to his eyes.

"How are you doing?" his grandfather asked, turning to William. "Did they manage to control your attacks?"

"Not entirely," William answered.

"Oh?" His grandfather glanced over at Goffman. He hesitated a bit before continuing. "Are you sure it's Cornelia?" Tobias whispered.

"Yes," Goffman said with a serious nod.

"How is that possible?"

Goffman shook his head. "We don't know."

William struggled. He wanted to tell them what he had

learned in the cave. That Cornelia was the third generation. Cornelia the Third. And that she hadn't come back
from the dead. She had been alive all along.

"How was the trip?" his grandfather asked, changing
the subject.

"Dramatic," Goffman said.

"I saw her on the plane," William said.

"Saw who?" Tobias asked.

"Cornelia," William said. "She caused the plane to
crash." He had to tell them something.

"That means that she sees you as a threat," his grandfather said, and gave William a serious look.

"Is that good?" William said.

"In a way," his grandfather said. "It means that she's
afraid that you might have a chance to stop her." He paused.
"But it also means that she's going to stop at nothing to get
you out of the way."

The group stood in silence, taking in the situation.

"Where's Iscia?" Tobias asked.

"One of the chauffeurs is out looking for her," Goffman
said. "She went missing in the snowstorm."

"Is she wearing an ultrasuit?"

"Yes," Goffman said.

"That's good. She'll be all right, then."

William glanced over at Freddy, who was still glaring
at him.

Tobias turned to William. "I found the entrance to where the Crypto Portal is located, but I can't get through it."

"I can try," William said.

His grandfather smiled tightly and glanced over at Goffman. "How long do we have until Abraham thaws?"

Goffman looked down at the cryogenic monitor.

"Thirty-six minutes," he said.

"Then we don't have any time to lose," Tobias said.

The elevator stopped, and the door rolled to the side.

# 29

The group moved through an underground tunnel deep inside the mountain. The structures surrounding them resembled the monastery they had seen on the ledge.

William wondered what it had been like back when people lived here.

Had there been kids like him? Would they have been playing in the streets?

William found the whole place fascinating.

"How long have you been down here?" William asked, looking up at his grandfather walking next to him.

"I came here the instant Benjamin gave me the coordinates," he said, fiddling with the memory stick hanging around his neck. William remembered seeing the object when his grandfather had picked him up outside school.

"We have known about the Crypto Portal for a long while," his grandfather continued. "But we didn't know where it was, and we thought that it must have been destroyed many centuries ago."

"Are there more underground cities like this?" William asked, looking around.

"Yes," his grandfather said as if that went without saying. "They're all over the world, but there's only one portal."

They stopped in front of a small stone door in the cave wall. Strange symbols were carved into it. Intuitively William knew what they meant. It said that anyone who entered should expect never to return. He felt a slight tremble in his stomach.

"Why haven't I had any attacks yet?" he asked, looking up at his grandfather.

"Now that the portal has been activated, it won't produce any more waves before Cornelia tries to send Abraham through it."

"And then?" William asked.

"Then you would get the most devastating attack. We have to stop her before she goes through with it." Tobias looked at Goffman. "How long before he thaws?"

Goffman looked at his watch. "Twenty-three minutes now."

"We have to get going. She can't send him through before he's thawed. We have to get William down there to deactivate the portal."

"But how?" William said, at a loss. "How do I deacti-vate it?" He didn't like the feeling of being responsible for the fate of the entire planet.

"As far as I know," Tobias said, "the only thing that can control the Crypto Portal is the orb that Cornelia has. Somehow or other, you're going to have to get it from her."

Tobias started moving separate parts of the door. Wil-liam followed his every move. His grandfather was an excellent code breaker.

"GET DOWN," Goffman yelled from behind them.

Instinctively William threw himself to the ground as a beam hit the wall right above his head. The stone wall seemed to turn to dust. William looked back: A figure was coming toward them.

It was Cornelia.

The chauffeur fired his passivator. The ray hit an invis-ible shield in front of her. She only flinched a little and continued.

"That damned hand of hers," Tobias said. He was still working on solving the door.

A new beam hit the wall, and his grandfather disap-peared in a cloud of dust. William heard him yell in agony.

"Grandfather?" William shouted.

"Over here," he shouted back.

William crawled over to the door and found his grand-father sitting up against the wall. He was clutching his leg.

"You have to solve the door," his grandfather said, his face twisted in pain.

William got to his feet. He could hear shouts from Goffman and the others. The zapping of lasers and passivators. It sounded like a full-fledged war behind him.

He *had* to concentrate if he was to solve the code and get his grandfather to safety.

William placed his hands on the door. The vibrations started in his stomach, then traveled up his spine and out into his arms. He could sense that this was a difficult code. However, he knew he could solve it . . . but could he do it in time?

"Hurry." He heard his grandfather moan.

William's hands started working. They moved the pieces around on the door. As one symbol after another fell into the right place, the door clicked from deep inside.

The last piece snapped into place, and the door slid open.

"I did it," William cried.

He grabbed his grandfather by the arm and helped him to his feet. They hurried in through the door as a blast hit the wall behind them.

William and his grandfather were flung forward and tumbled down a narrow stone staircase.

# 30

It was the sound, a strange mixture of deep rumbling and higher notes, that William noticed first.

William looked to the side and saw his grandfather on the floor next to him. He was covered in gray dust.

"Grandfather?" William said, and got onto his knees. He crawled over to him.

"I'm okay," Tobias said, and opened his eyes and forced a smile. "I've been through worse. Help me up."

William helped him into a sitting position. "Can you walk?" he asked.

"Of course," his grandfather said. "Give me a hand."

William helped his grandfather to his feet. He stood there for a few seconds, checking his balance.

"My leg is better now."

William looked up at the staircase. It was blocked by an avalanche of gray stones.

"The others are up there," William said. "On the other side."

"We can't afford to wait for them," his grandfather said. "While they're keeping Cornelia busy, we have to get to the portal. That's where Abraham is."

He motioned for William to follow and limped forward. It wasn't until this minute, as William's eyes adjusted, that he saw that everything around them was completely white. The walls, the floor, and the ceiling were bathed in a bright light.

"Where's the light coming from?" William asked.

"From the walls," Tobias replied. "Come on."

William looked around at his surroundings as they continued down a white hallway. Everything was so white that it was hard to see where the walls ended and the ceiling began. The floor felt weird; it didn't make a single sound as they walked. William stomped a little harder to test it, but it was as if the floor sucked all the sound away from his feet.

"How can this be many millions of years old . . . and look like a . . . spaceship from the future?" William stammered.

His grandfather didn't answer. They turned a corner and stopped.

"The portal is behind that," Tobias said, pointing to a

gigantic white door at the end of the room. "This is as far as I've managed to get."

William looked at the door. It was every bit as white as the walls, but it pulsed with a bluish light.

"It doesn't have symbols on it," William commented, "or a knob or handle. . . . There's no way to open it."

"You have to use that," his grandfather said, pointing to something.

William's eyes widened. Next to the door stood a massive robot that was so white it almost completely blended into the wall. He recognized it as similar to the one Iscia had shown him down at the Depository. Only this one was three times as big.

"It's an exoskeleton," his grandfather said. "It works on the same principle as the one your father has. We have found several of these around the world. And we have copied and developed the technology further, but this is still pretty advanced stuff."

"There's one like it at the Depository," William said.

"That's right," his grandfather said.

William walked over to the exoskeleton. He raised his hand and set it on the enormous foot. It was made of white metal and felt cold to the touch. A ladder continued all the way up the leg. It ended under a round indentation in the middle of the robot's chest. William could see a seat inside the hole.

"You want me to go up there?" he asked, pointing.

Tobias nodded. "I went up there myself and checked it out, but I couldn't get anywhere."

William turned back to the exoskeleton. He placed one foot on the bottom rung of the ladder and grabbed on to one of the higher ones.

He started climbing.

The combination of the weird sounds in the room and the lofty heights made him dizzy. He had to concentrate. He continued upward, one step at a time. It wasn't far now.

By the time William finally sat down in the white seat, sweat was pouring from his forehead. The seat was made of metal as well, but it was comfortable to sit in. It felt as if it were formed for his body.

"Now what?" he called down to his grandfather, who was looking up at him.

"Put your hands on the plates. There's one on either side of you," his grandfather called back.

William spotted a white glass surface on both sides of the chair's armrests. He positioned one hand on each plate. His hands sank down as the glass reconfigured around his fingers.

"Try moving the arms," he heard his grandfather yell.

William moved his right hand, and the large robot arm did the same. He tried the other hand, with the same result.

"Put your feet on the plates on the floor," his grandfather instructed.

William looked down at two glass plates on the floor in front of him. He put one foot on each, and his feet sank down into the material.

"Now you can make it walk."

William moved his feet, and the large exoskeleton did the same.

"Take a couple of steps toward me." His grandfather waved William over with both hands.

William moved one foot ahead of the other. The large metal construction jerked as it began to walk. He took a couple of steps toward his grandfather and stopped.

"Good. You've got the hang of it," his grandfather called out. "Now walk over to the door."

William turned the large exoskeleton and walked over to the white door, which was still pulsing with a faint blue light. He raised the robot's hands, splayed the fingers, and then placed them against the door. The surface immediately glowed blue around the large robot hands, and the high notes in the room changed.

"You need to use the notes to open the door," his grandfather said. "I've been trying for two days, but haven't gotten anywhere."

William looked at the massive robot hands in front of him.

"Why did they do it this way?" he said. "This thing is unwieldy."

"It's supposed to be unwieldy . . . and they were obsessed with tones and sound waves," his grandfather responded.

William moved one hand to another location on the white surface, and the tone of the high notes in the room changed again. He moved the other hand to another location. The notes changed yet again.

*This is like playing a piano,* he thought.

"I need to make a melody to open the door," he called out.

"Go on," his grandfather responded. "We don't have much time."

William closed his eyes and concentrated. He felt the familiar vibrations start and then begin to move up his spine and out into his arms and fingers.

When he opened his eyes again, he saw lights in all the colors of the rainbow dancing over the white door. He knew that the luridium was helping him solve the code and that the colors were something that only he could see. He moved the big robot hands and mimicked the movements of the colors in front of him.

At first there was no coherence to the sounds.

Then a melody emerged.

He played the melody, and the notes in the room played the same melody back at him.

William kept going, his hands working faster and faster.

He played it again and again. And the room played it back at him. It was like some weird musical battle.

Then the lights vanished, and the music faded away. And the room grew completely quiet.

William studied the wall in front of him, but nothing happened.

"What now?" he asked, and looked down at his grandfather.

"I'm not sure," his grandfather said.

William could hear uncertainty in his voice.

There was a rumble from deep within the door, and then it started moving downward, into the floor.

William moved the exoskeleton a couple of steps back. He stood there watching as the large white door disappeared into the floor under him, revealing a dark hallway on the other side.

# 31

**"We have to get in there,"** Tobias yelled, and limped toward the opening.

"What about the others?" William protested.

"We don't have time to wait for them," his grandfather said, and continued. "They'll get here when they've dug through the rubble."

William climbed down the ladder on the side of the exoskeleton's leg and jumped off the last rung.

He stopped and stood there staring into the darkness on the other side of the big door. Cornelia was inside there somewhere, waiting for him, but so was Iscia.

William continued into the hallway. He caught up with his grandfather, and Tobias turned on a little lamp on the top of his passivator. The lamp blinked on, lighting up the surroundings. They continued down the hallway.

William noticed that his grandfather limped badly now.

"How's your leg?" William whispered.

"Fine," Tobias said through gritted teeth. He swung the beam of light back and forth over the darkness. They were in a long narrow hallway that continued into the dark ahead of them.

"Do you know how to get to the portal?" William asked as they walked.

"No," his grandfather said, "but now that we're through the gate, it shouldn't be hard to find."

Suddenly William heard something . . . a rumbling. A dizzying, deep bass rumble. It made the floor tremble.

"What's that noise?" William asked, listening to the ominous sound.

"It's the portal," his grandfather said, stopping and pointing the beam of light into the darkness ahead. "There's something there," he whispered.

The light swept across two stone robots standing motionless at the end of the hallway. They looked like the exoskeleton William had used. Only these were smaller and granite gray in color.

"What are they?" William whispered.

"I'm guessing they're guards," Tobias said without taking his eyes off the robots. "If something happens, I'll try to distract them while you get to the portal."

They moved toward the two stone robots. Tobias kept his passivator aimed at them. William followed close behind him.

The robots didn't move. They stood there like two sculptures.

"Maybe they're inactive?" William whispered.

"Let's hope so," his grandfather whispered back, his voice trembling.

They stopped right in front of the robots and looked at them, but nothing happened. William felt himself relax a little. If they hadn't moved by now, they weren't—

Then, in an instant, both robots straightened up and came at them. The dust that had gathered on them over the eons floated into the air and made it difficult to breathe.

Tobias fired the passivator. The ray hit one of the machines, causing it to stagger backward for a moment before regaining its balance and continuing forward.

"Run!" Tobias yelled, pushing the passivator into William's hands. "I'll only slow you down."

"But—" William said.

"RUN! Now! Find the portal. Stop Cornelia!"

Tobias limped down the hallway in the direction they had come. The two robots clanked after him.

William turned and took off as fast as his legs would carry him. It was the first time he had held a passivator. It was much heavier than he had thought.

After running through the almost endless network of hallways, he stopped. His legs were trembling, and he could feel the adrenaline making every muscle in his body shake. He tried to quiet his breathing and listen.

The noise was much stronger now. The bass came at him from the floor and walls. It made his vision blurry.

He looked around as he struggled to keep his panic in check. Should he wait here for his grandfather or keep going?

His legs gave him the answer. It was almost as if they started walking on their own.

William proceeded down the hallway.

He turned a corner and stopped.

The endless stone walls now opened up into an enormous hall with a vaulted ceiling. In the center of the room he saw something he recognized immediately.

A large golden ring hovered above the floor. It was so high up that it was impossible to estimate how big it was, and it was so bright that it almost hurt to look at. But there was something hypnotic about it. William felt a strong attraction to it, as if it was calling to him . . . wanting him to come closer.

He felt gentle vibrations in his belly. Was that the luridium in him starting to move? Wanting to go through the portal?

William looked up at the hovering ring again. He knew what he was looking at. This was the Crypto Portal.

He forced himself to look away, and it was only then that he noticed what stood on the floor beneath the portal.

A white rectangular chest.

It was Abraham Talley's cryogenic freezer unit.

# 32

**There was a panel with a series of red blinking numbers on** the side of the freezer unit. The numbers were changing.

Counting down.

The display read 00:10:08.

Only ten minutes before Abraham thawed.

William's heart began to hammer in his chest, and a paralyzing fear spread through his body.

He looked up at the hovering ring. His thoughts returned to those beings full of luridium who had left earth all those years ago. Was that why he felt such a strong attraction to the hovering ring? Was the luridium in him trying to entice him to leave the planet? Maybe that wasn't such a bad idea? He wanted to stop fighting and give in, let himself be sent away. Maybe he would feel more at home wherever the portal led him.

"You feel it, don't you?" Cornelia said from behind him.

William whipped around, but there was no one there.

"Did your precious grandfather leave you in the lurch, William?" Cornelia asked. "And not for the first time, right? He's deserted you before, hasn't he?"

William didn't answer. Instead he raised the passivator.

"No matter what they tricked you into believing, William, you don't belong with them. And you know it. You're a machine. Not a human."

"I'M NOT A MACHINE," William yelled.

"Stop lying to yourself, William. You're different. You're not like the others."

"*Noooo,*" William yelled back.

"If you ever want to see your little friend again," Cornelia said, "you'll do as I say. Remember what we agreed."

William hesitated.

"Where's Iscia?" he asked.

"William," Cornelia said.

William turned around and saw her. She was standing a couple of yards away from him, watching with those wild eyes of hers. She held her leather bag in one hand.

"Where is she?" William asked.

Cornelia sneered.

"Let me see her!" he yelled. "Let me see Iscia!" He raised the passivator.

Cornelia looked over at Abraham's freezer.

"Not long now." She grinned. "Might as well have a little fun while we wait. Here she is."

Cornelia pushed various buttons on her mechanical arm and pointed it out into the room. A beam of light shot out and hit the floor, and the contours of a person began to materialize.

Soon Iscia was suspended in the air a little way beyond them. Her eyes were closed. And her head lolled to one side.

"Iscia!" William yelled, and started running toward her.

"Stop!" Cornelia screamed.

William pulled up.

"There's no point in yelling. She can't hear you," Cornelia continued.

"Show me that she's alive," William shouted. He pointed the passivator at Abraham's freezer. There was a glint of surprised fright in Cornelia's eyes.

"Okay," she said. "I'll play along for a bit. We have five minutes."

And once again she aimed her mechanical hand at the girl. When the next light ray hit Iscia, her body jerked.

"Iscia!" William called.

Iscia looked around the room with frightened eyes. Then she saw him, and their eyes met.

"William?" she said.

He wanted to run to her, but Cornelia seemed to know what he was thinking.

"Stay still," Cornelia yelled, waving a menacing hand at Iscia. "It will soon be time." She looked at the display on Abraham's freezer. "Now your pretty little girlfriend can watch as you make yourself useful."

"What's going on?" Iscia asked. Her voice was trembling.

"Open the lid on the freezer!" Cornelia aimed her mechanical hand at Iscia.

"Don't do it!" Iscia said. "You know what will happen if he makes it through."

With a loud zap Cornelia fired a blue beam that hit Iscia, causing her to slump to the floor.

"No!" William yelled.

Iscia moaned and grabbed her head.

"Next time I'll give her a lethal dose," Cornelia said. "Open the lid!"

William had no choice. He had to do what she said even though his whole body bristled at the thought. He walked over to the freezer unit.

"Do it," Cornelia ordered. "Turn the handle."

William raised his hand and grasped the chrome handle on the lid.

He glanced back at Iscia. Then he gulped and turned the handle to the side. When he did, there was a loud *FSSSSSSSSST* . . . as if the whole freezer were exhaling.

William took a couple of steps back, without taking his eyes off the unit. The lid jerked and then tipped open. A gray frosty mist poured out of the box, and a blue light blinked to life inside the smoke.

Inside the freezer unit, William could make out the contours of a body.

Abraham's body.

It lay there. Motionless.

William glanced over at Iscia.

Her eyes were red, and tears poured down her cheeks. William knew she would never forgive him if he helped Cornelia send Abraham through the portal, even if he was doing it to save her.

"Now what?" he said, turning to Cornelia.

"Move away," Cornelia said. "It's my honor to do the rest."

Cornelia came toward him, unzipping the leather bag. The little cockroach crawled out, scurried across her arm, and took refuge in one of her jacket pockets.

William felt the cold air coming from the freezer. He couldn't take his eyes off Abraham's body. It looked unearthly, surrounded by bluish frost smoke.

He had to concentrate to remain calm. He couldn't panic now or, even worse, have an attack.

Cornelia stopped in front of the freezer, took the orb out, and set the bag on the floor. She bent down and placed the orb on a round metallic plate set into the floor.

The instant the orb touched the brass, the large ring

above them began to spin, and a bright beam of light traveled from the ring down to the floor where the freezer stood.

Cornelia took a couple of steps backward, her eyes fixed on the freezer.

William's eyes were focused on the beam. He had to fight the urge to just walk into it and let it carry him away.

William felt the hum from the vibrating ring all around him. It had grown so powerful now that the floor shook under him. The vibrations traveled up his legs and into his stomach. William knew an attack was on its way.

The cold was spreading, creeping up his spine. Soon he would lose control of his body, and everything would be over.

Cornelia stood as if hypnotized. Her eyes were fixed on Abraham, who rose from the freezer and levitated horizontally along the bright beam, toward the vibrating ring. His eyes were still closed, and his whole body glowed.

# 33

**William glanced over at Iscia as she slumped back down**
onto the floor like she'd given up completely.

Cold poured through his body. The rumbling in his
belly increased. Soon the convulsions would begin.

He didn't even try to fight it. This time he was going
to let it happen. He didn't care anymore. He had signed
a death sentence for the whole planet, so he deserved the
pain that was about to overtake him.

William watched in disbelief as Abraham's body traveled
upward along the light beam.

Then the abdominal cramps hit him like a hard fist to
the gut.

His legs turned to jelly under him, and he dropped
to the ground. He lay there writhing in agony. William

gritted his teeth as his whole body twisted in pain. With an agonizing effort, he lifted his head and looked over at Iscia. He tried calling to her, but his mouth wouldn't cooperate.

Cornelia stood with her back to him, peering up at Abraham's body, which was now halfway to the portal ring.

William fixed his eyes on Cornelia's back. Should he give up? She had won anyway. He had a strong desire to close his eyes and just let the seizure carry him away.

Then something caught his attention.

The cockroach had crawled up from the pocket of Cornelia's jacket. Its antennas fluttered about in the air like two little swords. It seemed agitated.

And just like that, an idea materialized.

William remembered what Benjamin had told him in the lab. There was enough luridium in the cockroach to make William 50 percent machine. It would enhance his abilities, but the danger would be in not knowing in which direction he would tip. Would he become a machine completely? Or keep his human qualities?

William felt his whole body relax like it knew that he had already made the decision. It was his only chance now.

With effort, he struggled into a sitting position. He stayed there for a few seconds, looking at Cornelia and the cockroach standing on the edge of her pocket. William glanced over at Iscia. She was looking at him now, her eyes frightened and wide. She shook her head. It was like she knew what he was planning to do, and like she also knew the danger it represented for him.

William felt an intense anger growing inside him. He couldn't let Cornelia and Abraham win.

He had to fight!

He had to do everything in his power to prevent them from succeeding—even if it meant sacrificing himself.

He fought his way onto his knees. The pain was unbearable, but he forced himself up anyway. He staggered toward Cornelia, who still had her back toward him.

William stopped right behind her. Her full attention was on Abraham, who was two-thirds of the way to the ring now. It wouldn't be long before he would enter the portal ring.

Iscia sat up on her knees, following William with her eyes.

William put his index finger to his mouth, signaling for her to keep quiet.

Carefully he extended his hand. At first, the cockroach didn't seem to notice him. As William was about to grab it, it moved farther away on the edge of the pocket.

William felt his heart jump as the cockroach began shaking. Its seizure was also starting. Cornelia looked down and noticed the cockroach.

"Where are you going?" she said, and reached down with her hand. "Come here—you have to watch this."

With a quick grab, William snatched the insect and moved away, clutching it in his fist. He could feel it struggling to get free. It was strong for its size and vibrated powerfully now.

Cornelia whipped around.

"What are you doing, you little brat?" she barked. "Give it back!"

"No," William said, shaking his head.

"I said, GIVE IT BACK," Cornelia screamed.

His paralyzing pain was replaced with an intense anger.

Why should he let Cornelia tell him what to do? Why should he have to choose between Iscia and the world? He didn't care what happened to himself anymore. All he wanted was to get Iscia to safety and stop Cornelia from sending Abraham through the portal.

Cornelia raised her mechanical hand and pointed it at William, but she didn't fire. Instead she hesitated. Was the cockroach that important to her?

William opened his fist and looked at it. It had stopped shaking and lay completely still now.

"Give it to me," Cornelia said. Her voice was trembling with anger.

William ignored her and continued backing away, all his attention on the cockroach. Somehow, grabbing it had given him the upper hand.

Tiny silvery droplets started appearing on the cockroach's shell, almost as if it were sweating metal. The droplets seemed to be attracted to each other like liquid magnets. They clumped together to form larger drops.

This was exactly what William had hoped for: the luridium leaving the insect, attracted by the larger amounts of luridium in William's own body.

The luridium rolled from the cockroach and into his palm, then disappeared through the pores of his skin. And like that, it was gone. It was inside him.

He looked up at Cornelia, who was staring at him. It was as if time had stopped. Then William started shaking, and he could feel a surge of energy shooting through his body. And he knew that the luridium from the insect was merging with his own luridium. He looked down at the cockroach, which twitched and rolled over onto its feet. It jumped from his hand onto the floor and scrambled toward Cornelia. She bent down and grabbed it.

William knew what he had to do. He shot toward the orb under the golden ring.

He could hear Cornelia screaming, but her voice sounded muffled and far away. He looked over at her. She was coming toward him but seemed to run in slow motion, as if she were underwater. William looked up at Abraham, who had almost reached the ring now. He bent down and grabbed the orb.

The moment he removed the orb, Abraham's body stopped and hung there, suspended just below the golden ring.

William walked backward, holding the orb in his hands.

He realized he had gained control over his attack. Maybe it was due to the extra amount of luridium he had absorbed, or maybe it was willpower. The pain was gone, and he felt stronger and more focused than ever. But by the time he heard the footsteps, it was already too late.

Her face contorted in rage, Cornelia flung herself at him, hitting him full force. William lost his balance and fell over, clutching the orb with both hands.

He landed hard on his back with Cornelia on top of him. And then time returned to normal.

"Give me that!" she yelled, grabbing for the orb with her human hand.

She bared her brown teeth at him, and her rancid breath stung his eyes. Cornelia aimed her mechanical hand at his head. William remembered how the hand had moved around by itself on the plane and how Cornelia had twisted it back into place.

Then the hand made the loud beeping noise that meant it was charging for a powerful blast. He dropped the orb and grabbed her arm with both hands. The mechanical hand beeped louder and louder. He was going to be melted into the floor, just like poor old Pontus Dippel. He took a firm grip on the hand and twisted it around. First in one direction and then the other.

With a quiet click the whole hand came off.

"NOOOOOO!" Cornelia screamed, reaching for it with her other hand.

William crawled backward and got to his feet.

"GIVE IT BACK!" Cornelia screamed, rushing at him.

William aimed the hand at her and pushed all the buttons at the same time.

There was a loud zap, and a light ray shot out of it, grazing Cornelia's coat.

Cornelia hissed. "Who taught you how to shoot?"

William pressed the buttons again. A new beam shot out of the hand and hit Cornelia square in the gut. She was flung backward and slid across the floor. He stood there waiting for her to get back up and come at him again.

But she didn't move. Half her body was melted into the ground. Her eyes closed, head tilted forward.

Then the portal started humming again.

William looked around and saw Freddy standing by the freezer. The orb was back in its place on the floor, and Abraham's body ascended toward the spinning ring again.

"Freddy?" William shouted. "What are you doing?"

"She's in my head," he mumbled. "Make her stop."

"What are you talking about, Freddy?" William shouted. "Make who stop?"

"I'm sorry, William," Freddy said, and looked at him. His eyes were red with tears. "She made me trick you into solving the orb. . . ."

"Look," Iscia shouted. "It's happening."

William looked up at Abraham's body, which was glowing now as it entered into the spinning ring.

And then he was gone.

William couldn't believe what had happened. Abraham's body had gone through the portal. They had lost.

"William," he heard Iscia shout from behind him. "Freddy . . . Stop him."

William looked at Freddy, who was walking toward the beam of light under the portal.

"FREDDY," William shouted. "STOP!"

But Freddy didn't respond. He just kept moving forward.

"FREDDY!" William yelled. "Don't go any closer."

But Freddy kept going.

"What are you doing?" William started after him.

"Stop him!" Iscia called out.

Freddy stopped right in front of the beam of light and looked back. He cast a quick glance at Iscia. "I'm sorry," he said before proceeding into the light. His body jerked violently when it met the light. Then he went limp and fell backward into a horizontal position.

"Stop him," Iscia yelled as Freddy started to ascend along the beam just as Abraham Talley had done.

"No!" William called out.

He grabbed hold of Freddy's leg, but the force pulling Freddy toward the portal was so strong that William couldn't hold on.

He lost his grip and watched as the other boy's body disappeared into the golden ring.

William knew he had to act fast. He quickly bent down and picked up the orb from its place. The beam of light disappeared, and the humming stopped.

Everything was quiet.

He felt the vibrations start in his stomach.

It happened faster this time. In an instant, the vibrations shot up his spine and out into his arms. He had to deactivate the portal before anyone else went through it. Or worse, came back from whatever was on the other side.

The ancient symbols on the orb lit up and exploded into the air. They swirled around him like a school of playful fish, then broke apart into groups. Some of the symbols were smaller, others much bigger. They flashed in different colors and shapes. William knew which symbols to watch. He followed them as they sped around him and crashed into other symbols, forming new ones in small explosions.

William's hands started moving. Very fast. Faster than they had ever moved before. Was it the extra boost of luridium in his body that made him this quick?

It had to be.

His hands turned and twisted the old orb. The parts were hard to move at first. Then they eased up and became more cooperative.

In a moment he had solved the orb, and he had found a secret mode . . . somehow he just knew it. It would destroy the portal for good. William looked up at the portal as he backed away.

The huge ring stopped spinning.

The golden light faded away.

And with a thunderous bang, it fell to the ground, making the whole hall shake.

# 34

**William helped Iscia to her feet.**

"Can you walk?" he asked.

"I think so," she said.

Her legs wobbled as William supported her. They walked farther away from the wrecked portal.

"Is it over?" Iscia asked as William helped her sit down against the wall.

"I think so," William said. He looked over at the ring. Then at Cornelia's lifeless body sticking up from the stone floor.

"Is she dead?" Iscia asked.

"I don't know," William said. His eyes stopped at Cornelia's mechanical hand lying on the ground not far from her.

He looked up as he heard running footsteps behind him.

Goffman raced into the room. He was covered in sweat and dust.

"What's happened?" he asked in a trembling voice. "Where's Abraham?"

William shook his head.

"And Freddy? He ran ahead of us. . . ."

William was about to answer but stopped as his grandfather came into the room. He limped over and knelt next to William and Iscia.

"Are you two okay?" he asked.

William nodded.

"But Abraham . . . ," William started, then stopped. He didn't know what to say.

"You did well," his grandfather said, looking at the wrecked ring. "They won't be able to come back using that." He gazed at William with proud eyes. He seemed about to say more, when a movement behind him caught William's eye.

Cornelia was stirring. Her arm stretched out for something. The mechanical hand.

Before William knew it, he was on his feet, running toward her. It was like everything happened in slow motion again. He watched as she grabbed her mechanical hand, turned it, and pointed it at him. Then there was a bright flash of light as a beam shot toward him. The beam missed him, and he continued toward her. He had to get to her before she could fire again.

Then she did something completely unexpected.

She turned the hand toward herself . . . and fired.

With a flash of light, the beam hit her and she was gone. All that was left was the mechanical hand, which fell to the floor with a loud clank.

William skidded to a halt, looking in disbelief at the empty hole in the ground before him.

"William," he heard Iscia call out.

He turned, and his heart dropped as he saw his grandfather lying on the ground next to Iscia. His body was becoming transparent.

"Her beam . . . ," Iscia called out. "It hit him."

"No . . . ," William screamed as he raced back to his grandfather.

He threw himself to his knees and held his grandfather's head in his hands.

"Grandfather," he cried out.

"William," his grandfather whispered, pointing to the floor next to him. "My chain . . . the flash drive . . ."

William looked at the chain with the small flash drive.

"Take it," his grandfather said. "Hang it around your neck. It's yours now."

William pulled the chain over his head without taking his eyes off his grandfather. Tobias's body was almost completely transparent already.

"I'm sorry." William was sobbing now.

"You're going to have to manage without me," his grandfather said, smiling. "You have to continue the work I started and do everything in your power to stop Abraham from coming back."

"But how?" William whispered. "I don't know how. . . ." William didn't know what to say or do. He had so many questions he still wanted to ask his grandfather. So many things he wanted to talk to him about.

"The Institute will help you . . . ," his grandfather whispered.

William knew there was nothing he could do to save his grandfather now. Tears flowed down his cheeks as he watched his grandfather's face grow paler. He held his head, but he could see his own fingers through his grandfather's forehead.

"Never forget how much I love you, William," his grandfather said. "And how proud I am of you."

William felt his grandfather dissolve away in his hands. It felt like fine sand slipping through his fingers. The more he squeezed, the faster it seemed to happen.

"Grandpa . . ." He sobbed in anguish. "Don't . . ."

But his grandfather was gone.

William sat there stunned, staring at his hands, holding nothing but air. The floor where his grandfather had been lying was empty. He couldn't believe what had happened.

His grandfather was gone.

# 35

**William sat up and opened his eyes.**

His face was covered in sweat, and his breathing was labored, as if he had just sprinted up a hill. But he hadn't. As he looked around and took in his surroundings, he saw that he was on an airplane surrounded by people—very normal people.

It took another couple of seconds before he realized that they weren't in danger anymore. He remembered the trek back down the mountains. It had been himself, Iscia, Goffman, and the two chauffeurs. Goffman had taken William and Iscia to the airport and booked them on a commercial flight back to England.

William thought of his grandfather. It felt like a bad dream, and he didn't feel ready to think about it. So he thought about

Freddy. It was as if an invisible force had pulled him into the portal along with Abraham, and William hadn't been able to stop him. But at least the portal had been destroyed. Abraham wouldn't be able to use it to come back.

He looked down at his hands. He had managed to overcome his attacks, and he had survived the absorption of more luridium, but all of that was dwarfed by the huge dark cloud hanging over him because of his grandfather's death.

"This is your captain," said a voice over the speakers. "We have started our descent toward London and will be on the ground in approximately twenty minutes."

"Finally," said a voice above him. "You're awake."

William looked up and saw Iscia standing in the aisle next to him. She squeezed past him and dropped into her seat. She had a small bag of nuts in one hand and a carton of apple juice in the other.

"I thought you'd be hungry when you woke up," she said, holding up the items. "You've slept nonstop for eleven hours."

"Thanks," William said, and took the carton. He opened it and gulped down the sweet liquid.

When he had emptied the carton, he took the bag of nuts. He tore the bag open and poured the contents into his mouth. He was starving. He could feel the nuts pressing against the inside of his cheeks as he chewed. He must have looked funny, because Iscia giggled.

William swallowed and placed the empty bag and carton in the seat pocket in front of him. It felt like he had slept for years. He leaned over and looked out the window. Somewhere below him was London.

He remembered the flash drive his grandfather had given him. He grabbed at his chest but found nothing. The necklace was gone. He was hit by a wave of panic.

"I put it in your pocket," Iscia said, pointing at his jacket. It seemed like she understood what he was looking for. "You tried to pull it off in your sleep. I was afraid you would snap the chain."

William stabbed his hand into his jacket pocket and felt the small flash drive and chain. He relaxed and pulled it out, slipping it over his head and around his neck again.

They sat for a while in silence.

"I just can't believe it," William mumbled.

"What?" she said.

"That he's gone." William glanced over at her.

"I know," she said, and leaned back in her seat. "It's unreal. He was larger than life. The thought that he could actually die never even occurred to me."

"Yeah," William said.

William looked down at the flash drive.

"I wonder what's on it," he said, changing the subject. It was too painful talking about his grandfather in the past tense.

"You'll find out soon enough," Iscia said.

"What do you think happened to Freddy?" William asked, looking at her.

Her face grew pale, and she lowered her gaze.

"I just don't understand what came over him," she whispered. "It seemed like there was some other force that made him do what he did."

"Where do you think he is now?" William said. "With Abraham . . . or dead?"

"I don't hope he's dead," Iscia said, looking at William. "But I don't hope he's with Abraham, either."

William stared out the window again.

"I have a strange feeling we're going to see him again," he whispered to himself.

They sat in silence for a while.

"Are you going back?" William asked her. "To the Institute?"

"It's my home," she said with a flat smile. "I don't have anywhere else to go."

"Why?" William said. He felt bad for not knowing the answer.

"I'll tell you someday." Iscia turned her head to gaze out the window. "What about you? Are you coming back?"

"I don't know," William said, and scratched his head. "Now that my grandfather . . ."

William stopped talking. He sat for a while, pondering.

Maybe the Institute didn't want him back after what he had done to the Depository for Impossible Archaeology, and for failing to stop Cornelia from sending Abraham through the Crypto Portal.

"I think they need you more than ever," Iscia said. It was as if she had read his thoughts.

"Maybe."

Then she became serious. "Were you really going to go through with it?" she asked in a near whisper, almost as if she didn't want anyone to hear.

"With what?" William asked, even though he knew what she was talking about.

"Help Cornelia send him through the portal?" she said.

William just sat there, looking at her. He didn't know what to say.

"The whole earth is more important than me," she whispered.

"I know," he said. But deep inside he wasn't sure that he meant it. To him, Iscia was becoming one of the most important people in the entire universe.

Iscia looked at him. She seemed to be about to say something, when a little girl's voice interrupted her.

"I know who you are," the voice said.

William looked up and saw a girl's head sticking over the seat in front of them.

"Huh?" he asked, confused.

"I know who you are," the girl said once more. "I've seen you on TV."

And now it dawned on William what the girl was talking about.

He could feel his stomach tightening up. She must have seen him when he lost the puzzle challenge against Vektor Hansen.

"You're William Wenton," the girl said. "The world's greatest code breaker." The girl held up something William recognized immediately: the Difficulty. The toy puzzle he hadn't managed to solve during the TV show.

William just sat there and stared at the plastic cylinder as a wave of bad memories washed over him: His defeat. Vektor Hansen's gloating. His first attack. The fear and insecurity.

"Where did you get that?" William asked.

The girl looked at William like he had dropped down from the sky.

"At the toy store, of course," she said. "Everyone has one these days."

William looked around the plane. Many of the passengers were looking at him now. Some had their heads together and whispered.

"I've been trying for days now," someone said behind him.

William turned his head and saw a little boy standing in

the aisle next to him. He was also holding the Difficulty. "It's almost impossible to solve it."

"Yeah, it's hard," a man's voice said from somewhere in front of them.

William spotted a man in a suit a couple of seats away. He held up the toy and smiled.

"It seems like everyone does have one," Iscia whispered as she looked around the cabin.

"Can you solve mine?" the girl in front of William asked, and held up her Difficulty.

"Er . . ." William hesitated.

"Please," the girl pleaded.

William could feel his stomach tensing when he looked at the toy. It reminded him of that disastrous night on TV. Back then he didn't know what was behind his seizures. He did now. And he had taken care of that problem.

"Come on," said the boy in the aisle.

William looked at Iscia.

"Wouldn't hurt . . ." She shrugged her shoulders and smiled.

William could feel his pulse speeding up, and his body tingled.

"Okay," he said, and extended his hand toward the little girl.

She gave him the Difficulty.

William leaned back in his seat and looked at the plastic

cylinder. He looked up at the people around him. All eyes were on him, and an eerie silence had fallen over the cabin.

He looked down at the Difficulty again and thought of something. This stupid toy was the only code he hadn't managed to solve. Ever.

He closed his eyes.

The vibrations started immediately. They began in his stomach, like always. Then they traveled up his spine and out into his arms. Everything around him faded away, and soon the only thing he could see was the Difficulty.

The vibrations continued out into his hands and stopped. William couldn't feel anything for a few seconds. And for a moment he thought that the vibrations had stopped. That once again he would fail to solve that stupid toy.

Then the vibrations came back with a vengeance. And his fingers started to work. Faster and faster. Time and place faded out, and William was lost, deep in concentration.

The Difficulty was yanked from his hands.

William came to and glanced down. Had he dropped it like he had on the TV show?

But the Difficulty wasn't on the floor.

Then he heard it: The applause. The cheering.

William looked at all the people surrounding him. Most of them had their arms in the air and big grins on their faces. He looked over at Iscia. She smiled and patted him on the back.

The little girl who had given him the Difficulty had taken it back from him. She held it in the air and shouted, "HE DID IT . . . I KNEW HE WOULD DO IT!"

William looked at the toy. And the little girl was right. He had managed to solve it. All the sides were the same, and the cylinder had split into two pieces.

"And you set a new world record," the boy next to him said enthusiastically. He looked down at the mobile phone he held in his hand. "Thirteen seconds . . . Vektor Hansen's old record was more than a minute."

William had never thought that he could be this relieved at solving a plastic toy. But he was.

He was very relieved!

# 36

**William stopped in the doorway to his room.**

It was two hours since he had come home from the airport. He had spent a couple of days at the Institute for debriefing. And they had had a formal ceremony marking his grandfather's passing.

William's mother had spent most of the time hugging him and feeding him pancakes, while his father wanted to know everything about what had happened. Both were distraught at his grandfather's death, but equally happy to have William back safely.

Even if it had been only a week since he had been here, it seemed like years had passed. He felt different . . . more mature and surer of himself.

Tougher.

His gaze stopped at the old desk his grandfather had given him. William continued into the room and put his hand on the cool wood, stroking the surface with his fingers. And the strange marks and symbols Tobias had carved into it many years ago. Then he looked at the newspaper in his hand. He read the front page:

THE DIFFICULTY

NEW RECORD: 13 SECONDS

WILLIAM WENTON MAY BE A GENIUS AFTER ALL

VEKTOR HANSEN CLAIMS FOUL PLAY AND

DEMANDS REMATCH

William folded up the paper, pulled out one of the drawers, and put the newspaper inside. He sat on the chair and looked at the laptop on the desk in front of him. He grabbed the flash drive that still hung around his neck, lifted the chain over his head, and flipped off the cap. He placed the drive in the USB slot on the side of the computer and waited. His foot bounced up and down in excitement while he stared in anticipation at the screen.

But nothing happened.

It didn't even seem like the computer had registered that William had inserted the flash drive.

Maybe it had been corrupted? Ruined?

William waited a little bit more.

Still nothing.

He could feel the disappointment creep over him. He had hoped that there would be something on it that would make him feel better. Perhaps a message from his grandfather. A letter, or better . . . a video.

He removed the drive from the USB slot, waited a little, and plugged it back in.

Then he waited some more.

Still nothing.

William slammed the laptop shut in frustration and stood up. He turned and headed for the door.

"Where are you going?" a voice asked from behind him.

William stopped. He wasn't alone.

"You have to learn to be a little bit more patient," the voice said. The voice sounded like it came from someone who was stuck in a box.

Slowly William turned around. He didn't see anyone. He was still alone in the room. He looked at the laptop.

"Come back here."

There was something familiar about that voice.

It couldn't be.

"What are you waiting for?" the voice asked.

It felt like an electric shock shot through his body. It couldn't be. That was impossible.

He extended one hand toward the laptop and slowly

lifted up the screen. At first it was completely black. Then a familiar face appeared.

"You look startled," Tobias Wenton said, and smiled up at him.

"I . . . I . . . ," William stammered. He was so shocked, his mouth had stopped working.

"Can you hear me?" his grandfather said.

William nodded.

"Good," his grandfather said. "I was starting to worry the software had failed me."

"Software?" William said.

"Yes. My software."

"Yours?" William stammered. He was confused now. "What are you?"

"I'm me," his grandfather said.

"But how . . . ? You died," William said. It was weird saying it out loud.

Tobias looked a little gloomy, like William had said something he hadn't known.

"You can tell me how that happened later," he said. "I must have given you the flash drive then?"

Again, William couldn't do anything but nod.

"I've spent the last year digitalizing my brain," his grandfather explained.

"Does that mean that it's really you inside there?" William said.

"Of course. Right up until the moment I stopped backing the data up, which was about a week ago."

William just sat there, staring at his grandfather's face. It was like having him back again. Like having a video conversation with him over the Internet or something.

"So you're not really dead?" William said.

"Correct. It's still me. I just don't have a body . . . yet." Tobias smiled. William did too. "I gather you and the Institute need me for a little while longer?"

"Yes," William said, and laughed.

He needed his grandfather more than ever. He was family. And his all-time hero.

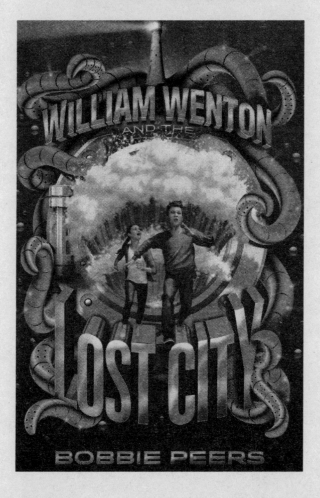

BIG BEN,
LONDON

**The world-renowned clock tower loomed darkly over the**
grand buildings. Gray moonlight was reflected in the clock
face. The gigantic hands said three thirty. London was quiet
now, so quiet that from down on the street you could almost
hear the clockwork inside the tower way up above. But in
the nighttime darkness the ticking was soon replaced by
something else.

Footsteps.

The dim light of a streetlamp revealed the shadow of a
person growing in time with the footsteps. At last a tall figure came into view and stopped in front of the fence surrounding Big Ben.

It was a man wearing a broad-brimmed hat and a long
overcoat. He glanced up at the clock face. For a moment

he stood completely still, like a statue on the dark street. Then, in one quick bound, he leaped the fence and strode over to the wall of the clock tower. He fumbled around in his pockets until he finally found what he was looking for: a small metal door no bigger than a matchbox. He ran a pale hand over the textured limestone wall, and as if the stone were magnetic, he secured the little metal door to it. With a series of clicks and mechanical movements, the metal door began to grow, becoming larger and larger until it was the size of a regular door.

The man glanced around warily before opening the door, stepping inside, and closing it behind him.

A short time later, the door opened once again, and the man emerged, holding something in his hands. It looked heavy and was wrapped in a dirty cloth.

He shut the door behind him. It shrank, and the man plucked it back off the wall. He returned it to his pocket and looked around before leaping back over the fence and vanishing into the darkness.

The sound of his footsteps faded away, and then there was complete silence. It was even quieter than before.

Big Ben had stopped.

In a secret control center at the Institute for Post–Human Research in England, a red alarm light started flashing. Beneath the light was a small label that said BIG BEN,

LONDON. A frightened technician looked up. He swallowed his coffee the wrong way and broke into a violent coughing fit, but his eyes remained transfixed by the flashing light the entire time.

"Call Goffman," he said, his voice quavering. "Now!"

**"William...," a voice said.**

William rolled over and pulled his pillow over his head.

"William . . . ," the voice said again. "You have to get up."

"Just a couple minutes," William grunted. "Just a couple more minutes."

"NOW, WILLIAM!"

He sat up and looked around. He had bed head, and his eyelids felt heavy. He glanced at the laptop on his nightstand. His grandfather's face smiled back at him from the screen.

"I'll be in trouble with your mother if I don't get you up on time," his grandfather said. "So you're going to have to get up no matter how tired you are."

"I know, I know . . . ," William mumbled, swinging his feet out of bed. The floor was cold, and he wanted to hide under his covers again. At the moment he thought his grandfather was lucky he was a computer program—he didn't have to wake up in the morning.

"You need to be out the door in nineteen minutes," his grandfather said.

William scrambled out of bed and found his clothes.

With both his mother and father at work, his grandfather was responsible for making sure William made it to school on time. Now that his father was able to get around without a wheelchair, thanks to the exoskeleton he had received from the Institute, he was working at the local museum. It was the same museum where William had cracked the world's most difficult code a little over a year ago, and had his life turned upside down.

"How many days are left now?" William asked, pulling his sweater on over his head.

It had become a ritual they performed every morning. William knew the answer but liked to hear his grandfather say it anyway. He could hardly wait to get back to the Institute.

"Eleven days," his grandfather said, smiling. "And you have fifteen minutes until your bus leaves. You should unplug me."

William walked over to the laptop.

"Have a good day," his grandfather said with a wink. "And keep out of trouble."

"You too," William said, and waved. He turned off the computer and pulled out the thumb drive.

Then he walked over to his grandfather's old desk and carefully placed the thumb drive in the drawer before taking out a small key and locking it.

Ten minutes later, William was running down the driveway in front of his house. He'd buttered a slice of bread at the last minute, and as he turned onto the sidewalk, he took a big bite of it, then stopped abruptly. A man wearing a red uniform and a hat that was pulled down so far the visor hid his face was standing in front of him. He held a small gray package in his hands.

"William?" he said.

William hesitated.

"William Wenton?" the man repeated, taking a step closer. He clicked as he walked. William glanced down at the man's shoes. They were white and black. Was he wearing tap shoes?

William looked around. There was an old, dented red mail truck parked in the street, but otherwise it was completely deserted.

"I have a very important express delivery for William Wenton," the man said. "Is that you?"

William forced himself to swallow the buttered bread in his mouth. "Yes," he eventually replied.

"Do you have some ID?" the mailman said.

"Uh." William thrust his hand into his pocket and pulled out his bus pass.

"You don't have one with a picture on it?"

"It says my name right there," William said, pointing.

The mailman muttered something to himself as he carefully tucked the package under his arm and inspected the bus pass.

"All right," he said after a moment, taking a step back. "I believe you. It's an honor to finally meet you, young Master Wenton." He bowed and tapped his shoes against the sidewalk a couple of times. Then he handed back the bus pass and held out the package. "Here you go."

William took it and was surprised at how heavy it was.

"What is it?" he asked, shaking the package a little.

"Careful," the mailman said. "It's supposed to be handled with care. And you need to be alone when you open it."

"Alone?"

William tried to look into the mailman's eyes, but the shadow from his visor still covered his face.

"Completely alone. This is not a dance for two."

William suddenly heard his bus down the street.

"I have to go," he said, and set out at a run for the bus stop.

"Handle with care!" he heard the man yell after him.

William reached the bus stop just as the bus doors slid open. As he climbed on, he turned and looked back toward his driveway. The mailman was still standing there staring at him, but by the time William found himself a seat and the bus drove past his house, the mysterious man was gone.

**Mr. Humburger paced back and forth in front of the board.**

"And when you hear the fire alarm . . ." He paused and eyed his students sternly. "Then you all stand up, nicely and orderly, and walk out the door in a line."

William sat in his seat and tried to concentrate on what his teacher was saying. But it was hard, since his thoughts were being constantly drawn to the strange package in his backpack.

"Then we'll gather by class out in the schoolyard and wait quietly for the fire department to arrive," Mr. Humburger continued.

There was going to be a fire drill. The students generally looked forward to these, because it meant a break from schoolwork. And today's would be extra exciting: The fire department was actually supposed to come.

Mr. Humburger glanced up at the clock on the wall.

As the second hand hit twelve, an alarm out in the hallway started wailing. Chairs scraped as the whole class stood up at the same time.

"No panic," Mr. Humburger urged as he directed the students with both arms.

William knew the teachers competed to see who could get their class outside first.

Mr. Humburger jogged over to the door and waved to his students. "Line up, everyone. Leave your backpacks here. We're coming back."

William leaned over and carefully lifted the package out of his backpack and hid it under his sweater. This fire drill suited him perfectly. No one would notice if he snuck off. He had to find out what the strange man had given him.

"Everyone, march in time with the beat," Mr. Humburger yelled. Then he placed a whistle in his mouth and started blowing the beat at the top of his lungs as he led the way out the door.

The whole class followed, marching down the hallway like a meager little parade for Norway's national holiday, the Seventeenth of May. As William's class moved along, other students started streaming out of their classrooms as well, and Mr. Humburger had to hurry. He sped up his whistling, and the marching students tried to keep pace.

William scanned the hallway. Now was his chance to

hide. The door to the teachers' lounge stood open, and the room was deserted. Glancing around quickly, he ducked out of line and snuck inside. Mr. Humburger's whistle faded into the distance.

William waited until it was totally quiet in the hallway. Then he walked over to the window and peered out. Three fire trucks drove onto the school grounds. Mr. Humburger was trying to direct them, but the drivers ignored him and parked in a completely different location.

Breathing a sigh of relief, William sat down on the sofa. He placed the package on the coffee table in front of him and stared at it for a few seconds.

Scooting to the edge of the cushion, William untied the twine and started carefully removing the thick gray paper. He remembered what the mailman had said: The package had to be handled with care.

His heart beat faster. There were multiple layers of paper, but slowly something began to come into view.

A metal pyramid.

It was covered with strange geometric figures that pulsed with white light.

The familiar vibrations began right away. They started in his belly before continuing up his spine. In William's head the symbols on the pyramid began to come loose from the metal surface and hover in the air in front of him.

A code.

The pyramid was a code!

William quickly leaned back on the sofa, and the hovering symbols fell back into place. He wanted to solve it, but he was scared. The last time he'd solved a code without knowing what it did, he'd activated a portal in the Himalayas. William wasn't planning to make that mistake again. He had to talk to his grandfather before he did anything at all. He was about to wrap the pyramid back up when the door flew open, and Mr. Humburger stormed in.

"There you are!" he yelled. "We lost the lineup competition because of you. What are you doing in here, anyway?!" Then he spotted the pyramid. "And what is that?"

Before William had a chance to respond, Mr. Humburger snatched it from him.

"No, be careful . . . ," William protested.

The pyramid started emitting sparks, and Mr. Humburger screamed and dropped it back onto the coffee table.

"What's it doing?" he yelled, staggering backward. "Make it stop!"

He stumbled into the wall and remained frozen there.

The pyramid kept sparking as it vibrated its way across the table. William reached for it, but it fell onto the floor and kept going toward Mr. Humburger.

"What does it want?" Mr. Humburger yelled, pressing himself against the wall. "Why is it after me?"

"I don't think it's after anyone," William said, standing up.

The pyramid stopped vibrating and lay at Mr. Humburger's feet.

Sweat was pouring down the man's face, and he was opening and closing his mouth like a goldfish.

"Don't touch it," William said, edging cautiously closer.

"There'll be consequences for this, William," Mr. Humburger snarled. "Is it finished?" He stretched his foot out and kicked the pyramid.

"No, wait," William said.

The pyramid emitted a deafening howl, and a geyser of sparks shot out of it.

Mr. Humburger was in a complete panic now. He jumped over the pyramid, sprinted to the window, and yanked it open. He stuck his head out and yelled at the top of his lungs: "ALARM, ALARM!"

Everyone who was standing down in the schoolyard looked up.

"THERE'S A FIRE . . . THERE'S A REAL FIRE UP HERE!"

A fireman holding a firehose turned and pointed the hose at the window.

Mr. Humburger gasped for breath and tried to yell again, but the effort and his panic had drained the air out of him. He settled for flailing his arms around wildly.

A powerful jet of water shot out of the firehose and hit Mr. Humburger in the chest with tremendous force. He was flung backward and landed on his back a little way from the window. William ran over and tried to help him up, but Mr. Humburger pushed him away and scrambled to his feet on his own.

"I have to get out," Mr. Humburger yelled, pulling off his drenched T-shirt. "I have to get to the roof."

"No, that's dangerous!" William yelled, but the man didn't pay any attention.

"I need to buy myself a little time. I've been practicing this," he said; then he pressed his wet T-shirt to his face and ran out into the hallway.

William stood there. He turned and looked at the pyramid, which now sat completely still on the floor.

# CHARLIE HERNÁNDEZ

must navigate a world where *calacas* wander the streets, *brujas* cast spells, and things he couldn't possibly imagine go bump in the night. That is, if he has any hope of saving his missing parents . . . and maybe the world.

# Middle school is hard.

Solving cases for the FBI is even harder.
Doing both at the same time—well, that's
just crazy. But that doesn't stop Florian
Bates! Get to know the only kid who
hangs out with FBI agents *and*
international criminals.

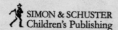